'Come on, Deputy Le[...]
what Chuck Willard say[...]

'No, but I'm sure you'[...]
murmured.

'Not just tell you. I'll show you!' I said.

CHUCK'S PEP TALK

Impossible? Nonsense. Add a gap and an apostrophe,
and what do you get? I'm possible.

'I'm possible?' said Nilesh. 'That makes literally no
sense.'

'Never mind,' I said. 'We have to get started
right now if we're going to have any chance. As I
mentioned in my speech, we need to target the non-
popular kids—I'm talking the emos, the chess club,
the metalheads, the boys' choir. We need to find out
what they want and promise to give it to them. We
have to give a voice to those with no voice, or in the
case of the choir, those whose voice is freakishly high
and girl-like. And try to get me some coverage on
Lowes Park Bantz. It seems like it holds a lot of sway.'

This book is dedicated to you, because you are AWESOME.

OXFORD
UNIVERSITY PRESS

Great Clarendon Street, Oxford OX2 6DP
Oxford University Press is a department of the University of Oxford.
It furthers the University's objective of excellence in research, scholarship,
and education by publishing worldwide. Oxford is a registered trade mark of
Oxford University Press in the UK and in certain other countries

Text copyright © Ben Davis 2018
Illustrations copyright © Mike Lowery 2018

The moral rights of the author have been asserted

Database right Oxford University Press (maker)

First published 2018

British Library Cataloguing in Publication Data

Data available

ISBN: 978-0-19-274796-9

1 3 5 7 9 10 8 6 4 2

Printed in Great Britain

Paper used in the production of this book is a natural,
recyclable product made from wood grown in sustainable forests.
The manufacturing process conforms to the environmental
regulations of the country of origin.

BY THE BRILLIANTLY FUNNY
BEN DAVIS
ILLUSTRATED BY MIKE LOWERY

MAKE ME AWESOME!

OXFORD
UNIVERSITY PRESS

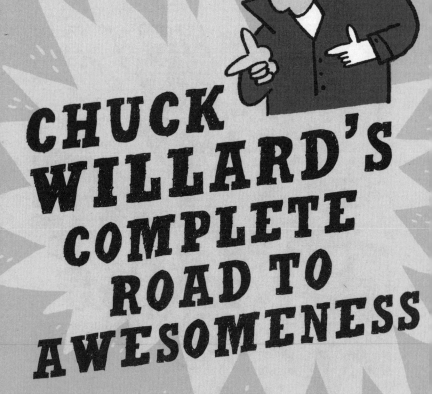

CHUCK WILLARD'S COMPLETE ROAD TO AWESOMENESS

Hi, I'm Chuck Willard—life coach, inspirer, giver of dreams. Thank you for joining my **COMPLETE ROAD TO AWESOMENESS PROGRAM**—the only program that puts you on the path to wealth, success, and most importantly, **AWESOMENESS**.

To adapt an old phrase: Some are born **AWESOME**, some achieve **AWESOMENESS**, and some have **AWESOMENESS** thrust upon them. I see it as my job to thrust upon you as much **AWESOMENESS** as I can. By the time you're through, you'll be stuffed with so much **AWESOMENESS**, you'll be bursting at the seams.

To get us started, fill out this questionnaire, then hit **SEND**.

NAME:	Frederick Michael Smallhouse
NICKNAME:	Freddie (me), Bum Breath, Badger Hair (various kids at school)
AGE:	13
OCCUPATION:	Um, school student, I suppose
ANNUAL SALARY:	My mum used to bung me a fiver every now and then

SEND

Wow, you sound **AWESOME** already, I don't think you need me! Just kidding. Please don't leave.

Now, in the box below, tell me more about where you are now and where you want to get to. Be as descriptive as you can. Heck, you can even draw pictures if that floats your boat.

★ 1 ★

Well, Chuck, I'm joining your **COMPLETE ROAD TO AWESOMENESS PROGRAM** because I'm desperate. This last year has been the worst ever for the Smallhouse family.

It all started to go wrong when Dad quit his job at the insurance company and set up his own antiques business. He was always into antiques— everything in our house was about a million years old and probably haunted by poltergeists. But the business was always a risk. Dad was nearly the boss at the insurance company and making good money. He had to take out loads of loans to open the shop and it went bust within a year. All we have to show for it now is an ugly suit of armour nobody wanted to buy.

But that's not the worst part, Chuck. To pay off Dad's debts, we had to sell our house. Our lovely house on Hyacinth Avenue where I had a nice big bedroom and a huge TV. And we've moved in with Uncle Barry. Yes, boring old Uncle Barry who works for the council and smells like Scotch eggs.

His house is SO much worse than our old place. My room is basically a cupboard. Instead of friendly neighbours like old Mr and Mrs Jennings there's a bloke called Heavy Metal Steve. Instead of a park at the end of the street, there's a rubbish tip.

You get what I'm trying to say, Chuck. It's not Awesome at all.

And here's the real kicker—we could be out any day now. Uncle Barry is selling the house, because he's moving to Germany for a dream job with the civil service. Yes, that's been his dream job since he was a kid. Not a rock star, not a footballer, a desk job in the most efficient office in the world. I don't get how we're related.

As soon as he goes, we'll basically be homeless, because our only other family is my grandad, but he lives in an old folks' home and we can't exactly set up camp there. It's OK though, because Uncle Barry has reassured us that he'll find a lovely B&B for us to sleep in before he goes. That's right, Chuck. A B&B. With a bathroom we have to share with ten different people.

Mum is trying to put a brave face on things, but it's not working. Even though Uncle Barry is her brother, they're not really alike. Uncle Barry is kind of mean. He's always switching lights off. Even if you're trying to read or write or sit on the toilet.

But the worst thing is, Dad just isn't Dad any more. He's always been super positive about everything. Even when our house was flooded.

WHOO, I LOVE SWIMMING!

But now, he's miserable. To make ends meet, he's had to get a job at a police dog kennel. His jobs include mucking out the pens and testing the protective padding they use to train the dogs.

Mum says that what with her job working
for the photocopier company, and Dad being
attacked by German Shepherds for a living, it will
take us years to get our own place again. This
means the B&B is definitely happening.

I had no idea what to do. Until about a week
ago, when the solution fell right into my lap.
Dad was flicking through the channels when he
came across your TV show, *How I Became Awesome
And You Can Too*. He didn't want to leave it on.
He reckoned it was a load of old rubbish and that

your teeth were unnaturally large and white, like a donkey, but I made him. Well, I say 'made', I actually waited until he went to the toilet then took the batteries out of the remote.

As soon as your show finished, I watched it again on +1 (Dad had gone to bed at this point) and I really took in everything you said. It left me feeling more hopeful than I have in ages.

'Your road to Awesomeness begins with a single step,' you said. 'Now put on your walking boots and get going!'

It wasn't just what you said, either, it was how you said it. It was as if you were staring out of Uncle Barry's rubbish telly and into my soul. I knew right away that if anyone can save my family it's you.

As soon as the show finished, I raided my life savings (£32.54) and used them to buy a six-month pass for your **COMPLETE ROAD TO AWESOMENESS PROGRAM**. With your **AWESOME** help, Chuck, all our problems will be solved in no time.

SEND

★ 6 ★

That sounds **AWESOME**! I will now analyse your answer and put together a package of **AWESOME** hints and tips to get you on the fast track to **AWESOME TOWN**.

REMEMBER: You should fill in your **JOURNAL OF AWESOMENESS** as often as you can. It's a cool way of keeping track of your progress. Now go get 'em, Slugger. The world is your oyster.

HOW TO MAKE YOUR BUSINESS AS AWESOME AS IT CAN BE

★

ENTREPRENEUR—the best word in the English language. I am one of the world's finest entrepreneurs. I started my business selling jeans out of the trunk of my car and now I'm a multi-millionaire selling dreams out of the trunk of my mind. And I'm here to tell you that it can happen for you, too!

Here are three key things you'll need to turn your business from shoestring to **CHA-CHING!**

1 IMAGINATION

You gotta think outside the box and not be afraid to take risks. People laughed when I started yelling positive thoughts into bottles and selling them online, but two million dollars later, the only one laughing is your old buddy, Chuck.

2 A NEVER-SAY-DIE ATTITUDE

The word 'quit' does not even exist to me. This mindset pulled me through after I came down with malaria after being bitten by a mos----o.

3 RUTHLESSNESS

In the cut-throat world of business, it's dog-eat-dog, and you need to be the biggest pooch in the pound. Friends, family, and community are nice ideas, but totally useless in your quest to be the big kahuna. When you're a millionaire, you'll have more friends than you can shake a diamond-encrusted sceptre at.

And that's it! Just follow these three simple rules, and I will be seeing you at the Rich Guy Club in no time. Mine's a slimline soda!

Yours Awesomely,

Chuck

Here we go, the first entry in my Journal of Awesomeness.

If I'm going to get us out of this mess, I'm going to have to become an entrepre . . . an enterpun . . . a businessman. Or at least, Dad is. If I can get an idea off the ground, then get Dad involved, there's no reason we can't succeed. Plus, as a side-effect, it would get him out of his slump.

It didn't get off to the best start. Dad was all 'Leave me alone' and 'I'm not interested' and 'For God's sake, it's 7 a.m. on a Saturday morning'.

When he'd finally got up and had his morning coffee, I tried again.

'I'm serious, Dad,' I said. 'This idea couldn't possibly go wrong.'

Dad didn't look up from his paper, where he was blackening the Prime Minister's teeth with a stubby pencil he'd nicked from Argos. 'Shows what you know, son,' he said. 'Everything can go wrong. And in my experience, it will.'

My stomach twisted. It's weird seeing Dad so low. He would never dismiss stuff out of hand before. Dad always put a million per cent into everything. I remember when we were on holiday and he bought us a dinghy for the beach and wrote SS *Smallhouse* on the side of it. I mean, yeah, he went a bit too far when he smashed a bottle of champagne on the side and burst it, but that's not the point.

'No, listen,' I said. 'I had this idea just yesterday. See, the offy always has a Choc of the Week, which they sell for 20p each. I say we go in, buy all of them, then sell them on for full price.'

Dad sighed. 'So we make a 30p profit on each bar?'

I nodded.

'And how many bars do they usually stock?'

'About twenty.'

Dad looked up from his paper for the first time. His eyes were as baggy as the swimming trunks I was promised I would grow into.

'We'd make six pounds a week,' he said. 'I don't

think I'll give up the day job just yet.'

Mum slid her bowl of cereal onto the table and sat down. 'Come on, Brian, be nice. That's a lovely idea, Freddie. It shows an enterprising spirit.'

'Thanks,' I said. 'I learned it from Chuck Willard.'

Dad groaned and called you a 'daft old horse-faced huckster', but I ignored him. He'll come around eventually.

Uncle Barry, who until now had been sitting silently, cutting coupons for wiener schnitzels out of a magazine, decided to speak up.

'Do not even think about starting that business, Frederick,' he droned, in a voice that sounded like he permanently had tissue wedged up his nose. 'If you do, you will be contravening Tammerstone Borough Council Business Regulations Section 25, Paragraph 6, and I will have no choice but to issue you with a £30 fine.'

Dad threw his tiny pencil down. 'So that's how you carry on not fixing potholes, is it, Barry? You fine kids?'

Uncle Barry pointed at Dad with his coupon-snipping scissors. 'The law is the law, Brian. One must always be diligent in life. If you had, perhaps you wouldn't be in your current situation.'

'Anyway,' Mum chirped, probably sensing that something was going to kick off. 'What's everyone up to today? They're showing a Bond film on TV this afternoon.'

'That's it,' Dad barked, scraping his chair as he stood up. 'I'm going out.'

'But Brian, you're still in your onesie,' said Mum.

Dad yelled 'Whatever', then stomped out of the house, slamming his tiger tail in the front door in the process.

CHUCK'S PEP TALK

When you're a leader, you have to take care of your men.

If one of your troops is off message, you have to inject them with an emergency dose of **AWESOMENESS**.

BAM! Straight into the heart.

LEGAL NOTE: This is a metaphor. Do not inject anyone without their permission.

I pulled on my trainers and ran after Dad. He was halfway up the road by the time I caught up with him.

'Is it OK if I come with you?' I asked him.

He side-eyed me and said, 'OK. I don't know why you'd want to spend time with an old loser like me, though.'

I couldn't believe what I was hearing, Chuck. My dad isn't a loser, he's just unlucky, that's all. That was when I had an idea.

'Shall we go for a game of mini golf?' I said. We always used to go there and Dad loved it. Once we'd had a quick round of that, Dad would be up for joining me on the road to Awesomeness, I knew it.

Half an hour later, he was whacking a giant plaster clown with his club.

'I always used to get a hole-in-one here,' he cried. 'What's happening to me?'

I looked at our score card. I was beating him. And I was eight over par, too.

'It's all right, Dad,' I said. 'It's not the winning, it's the taking part that counts.'

'Stop trying to make me feel less of a loser, son,' said Dad. 'I know you mean well, but we have to face facts.'

'Smallhouse, is that you?'

Dad screwed his eyes shut and turned around. It was Malvern Pope, a bloke he used to work with at the insurance company. When Dad left, he was promoted to manager. With him was his son, Malvern Pope Junior, the most popular kid in my year. Since we sold our house and moved in with Uncle Barry, he's been winding me up all the time, calling me names like 'Tramp Boy' and 'Bin Dipper' and 'Smallhouse from the small house'. They were wearing matching jogging gear.

'Hello, Malvern,' Dad mumbled. 'Fancy seeing you here.'

'Sorry to hear about the antiques shop, old sport,' said Malvern Senior. 'It's like I told you— not everyone likes crumbly old stuff as much as you do. Nice outfit, by the way.'

Dad looked down as if he was surprised he was wearing the onesie, then blushed. 'This is, um, actually more of an around-the-house thing.'

Malvern Junior put his hand to his mouth to stop his laughs and with his other, took his phone out of his arm holster and snapped a quick photo of Dad.

'Things are better than ever at MorganKemptonSchneffleBerger,' said Malvern Sr. 'Just got a nice little bonus in the old pay packet.'

'Isn't that something?' Dad grizzled.

'Yep,' Malvern went on. 'That £20k will come in handy when the new Merc is on the market.'

I could actually hear Dad grinding his teeth. That could have been our bonus. And our Merc.

'Great,' said Dad. 'Well, I'll see you around, Malvern.'

'Yeah,' said Malvern Sr. 'Hey, if you ever fancy a round of the real stuff, I'm a member of the Country Club, so I could get you in. Probably best not to dress like Tigger though, eh?'

Then he and Idiot Jr laughed and jogged away.

'So,' I said to Dad, trying to ignore what had just happened. 'What shall we do now?'

Dad ran his hands down his face. 'I think I might go to bed and never get up.'

CHUCK'S PEP TALK

Remember: If Plan A doesn't work out, make sure you have a Plan B. If Plan B doesn't work out, make sure you have a Plan C. Keep going 'til you reach the end of the Awesome Alphabet, buddy!

PLAN B

So it wasn't the best start I could have hoped for, Chuck, but I wasn't about to give up that easily. While Dad headed home with his tail quite literally between his legs, I decided to stay out and look for inspiration. Maybe I could get my business started on my own. Then I'd show Dad how much money can be made when you have an Awesome outlook.

I started off by asking Señor Whippy the ice cream man if he had any tips on breaking into the food business, but he was all, 'You buyin' a 99 or what, you little grotbag?'

Then I remembered it's market day in town, so I headed there. I know you got your start selling clothes somewhere like that, so I thought it would be a good place to begin. Maybe I could sell all the old clothes I'm too big for.

After the market lady told me she wouldn't give me anything for my 'dirty old kecks', I found

myself outside the Safebuy supermarket, and
THAT was where I found my Plan B.

How about that, Chuck? Is that a sign, or what?
I mean, yes, it was literally a sign in the window,
but you know what I'm trying to say.

But I knew I couldn't do it alone, especially since we've only got until tomorrow to get our entry in. It reminded me of a plan me and my best mate Nilesh came up with a while ago, so I headed over to his house. We meet up most weekends anyway, to play Epic Warfare on the Xbox. We've played it competitively before and came third in the regional finals. It even got mentioned on the school's Instagram gossip account.

@LOWESPARKBANTZ Pair of losers lose

It's always a bit of a bummer going to Nilesh's house because he lives near our old place and it just reminds me that I have to go back to Uncle Barry's palace of rubbish. I tried not to think about it and concentrate on my mission.

'What do you mean you don't want to play Epic Warfare?' Nilesh said to me at his front door. 'Have you got something wrong with you? If you have, you can stay out. I don't need your lurgy.'

'What a welcome,' I said. 'No, I just thought we could do something else.'

Nilesh frowned warily. 'You want to play Switchyswitch?'

I shook my head. 'Nope. I don't want to play Switchyswitch.'

I should explain, Chuck—Switchyswitch is an outdoor game we invented. We sneak into the front garden of Nilesh's next-door neighbours, the Barringtons. We then change their TV channel with Nilesh's long-range universal remote which works on everything. Seeing how annoyed Mr Barrington gets is amazing. The best was when we were having a sleepover and we turned

the rude channel on just as Mrs Barrington was
walking into the room with a plate of biscuits.

'So what do you want to do?' Nilesh asked.

'Become Awesome, my friend,' I replied.

He facepalmed. 'Are you really serious about
that Chuck Willard mumbo jumbo?'

'One: it is not mumbo jumbo, and two: yes

I am,' I said. I've been trying to convert him at school, but so far, he's not having it.

'Then leave me out of it,' he said. 'I don't have the energy for any "Awesomeness."'

'OK,' I said, pulling a SnackStars flyer out of my pocket and shoving it in his face, 'but do you have the energy to earn a hundred thousand big ones? This could be the thing that saves my family!'

Nilesh read it, then looked at me like I was crazy. 'What are we supposed to make for this?'

'Come on now,' I said. 'Don't you remember our business idea?'

Nilesh cocked an eyebrow at me. 'You mean the Indian food business that sells authentic snacks based on my nan's recipes, as an alternative to packaged supermarket rubbish?'

I nodded. 'We're setting up Proppadums.'

Nilesh puffed out his cheeks. 'I don't know, man. My nan is massively secretive about her recipes. She says that if you want them you'll have to kill her.'

'We won't need to kill anyone,' I said, 'when we have Chuck.'

Nilesh huffed as I took my tablet out of my bag. 'Don't tell me you've actually signed up to his program.'

'Listen to this,' I said, ignoring his negativity.

CHUCK'S PEP TALK

No one should stand in the way of your Awesome business, and if people around you can't get with the program, you don't need 'em!

'Oh my God, you DO want to kill her,' Nilesh gasped.

I laughed and clapped my hand on his shoulder. 'I'm not saying that at all, I'm just suggesting that we if we want to progress, we have to use our imagination.'

Nilesh eyed me suspiciously. 'What do you mean, "imagination"?'

'Chuck calls it "thinking outside the box",' I said. 'And I must be a natural at it. Like, when we were on the plane to Tenerife a couple of years ago, my mum paid a tenner for an inflatable neck pillow. I found one—totally free—under my seat.'

Nilesh's mouth dropped open. 'Wasn't that a life jacket?'

I shrugged. 'Don't care what it was, it did the job. Plus, I was able to alert the attention of the cabin crew by blowing the cool whistle that was attached.'

'You have got to be kidding me,' said Nilesh. 'They tell you not to inflate those things until you leave the aircraft. If that plane had crashed, you could have stopped people getting out in time, you idiot.'

I tapped my temple with two fingers. 'Imagination.'

'I don't know,' said Nilesh. 'It seems like a lot of work.'

'Oh come on,' I said. 'You know how much I need money right now. The other day I had to darn Uncle Barry's socks for three quid.'

Nilesh shuddered.

'And maybe, when me and my family are in our own house and we're rich, you and me can branch out and invest our money into something really cool,' I went on.

Nilesh gasped. 'Are you talking about our monkey hotel?'

I nodded. It was a plan we've had since we were five. A hotel staffed entirely by monkeys. Monkey receptionists, monkey chamber maids, monkey waiters. Once we'd paid them in bananas and tyre swings, the rest would be sweet, sweet profit.

After I got Nilesh onside, we headed to the kitchen to try and get the recipe. With how miserable Dad was after being caught dressed as a tiger by Malvern Pope Sr, I couldn't afford to waste time. We found Nilesh's nan cooking lunch in a big pot, while his Mum and Dad sat at the kitchen table.

Nilesh went up to his nan and asked if she wouldn't mind sharing some of her recipes. She turned around and snarled, 'THESE RECIPES WILL REMAIN WITH ME UNTIL THE DAY I DIE!'

I glanced over at Nilesh's parents but they seemed really interested in their newspapers. It wasn't going well. Time for me to step in.

'Mrs Biswas,' I said. 'We believe that your recipes are so delicious that they deserve a wider audience, don't you agree?'

Nilesh's nan scowled at me for what felt like ages, then looked at Nilesh and said, 'Who is this fool?'

'It's Freddie, you know it's Freddie,' said Nilesh. 'Now, please, just your samosa.'

She slapped him on the forehead with a spoon, leaving a massive splat of sauce hanging there.

'No,' she barked. 'I will only reveal my recipes on my deathbed. To your mother. Until then, HANDS OFF!'

Nilesh wiped his forehead with a cloth and followed her across the kitchen. I made sure to keep my distance. I had spent ages doing my hair and didn't want to get food in it.

Nilesh's nan took a jar off the shelf and peered at us through her thicker-than-triple-glazing glasses.

She said, 'You remind me of myself when I was your age—always pestering my mother for her recipes, wanting to know her secret. And do you know what she would say to me?'

We shrugged.

She snarled and growled a long sentence that made absolutely no sense. I looked at Nilesh, but he was as clueless as I was.

'And, um, what does that mean?' Nilesh asked.

'IT MEANS MIND YOUR OWN BUSINESS!' she growled.

Nilesh turned to his parents and said, 'Mum, Dad, what did Nan really just say?'

Nilesh's mum wrinkled her nose and said, 'I'll tell you when you're eighteen.'

Anyway, Chuck, although we hit a roadblock on our road to Awesomeness, that doesn't mean we won't get there. It just means we'll have to take the diversion.

CHUCK'S PEP TALK

Shoot for the moon. Even if you miss, you'll land among the stars. And do you know what the nearest star is? The Sun.

Hot stuff!

We waited in the lounge for Nilesh's nan to go out to her social club. Then we looked in the fridge.

'Do you see what I see?' I asked Nilesh.

He said, 'A samosa?'

I laughed. 'You may see a samosa, my friend, but what I see is an opportunity.'

Nilesh leaned closer and squinted. 'Nah, that's definitely a samosa.'

I picked it up and sniffed it. Nilesh said, 'Ugh, I was going to eat that later.' I shushed him and took another drag.

'If your nan won't share her recipe, then we must try to replicate it,' I said.

Nilesh said, 'I don't know, mate, I don't think she'll be happy about that.'

'She doesn't need to know, does she?' I said.

'Even if you're right,' said Nilesh, 'how are you supposed to replicate that samosa?'

I slammed the fridge door and pointed to the exit. 'To the lab!'

Nilesh looked confused.

'My bedroom,' I said.

We headed over to my house. It's always a little embarrassing going from Nilesh's to mine, but we had to if we wanted to work on our samosa without the risk of his nan coming back and killing us to death.

When we arrived at my house, I could hear Heavy Metal Steve in his shed, having a 'jam session' with his band, Furious Gibbon. Uncle Barry was in the lounge, brushing up on his conversational German.

We hurried to the kitchen and closed the door. I carefully unwrapped the samosa and laid it on the worktop.

'What we are attempting is a very delicate procedure,' I said to Nilesh. 'Scalpel, please.'

Nilesh pulled a pair of E-Z Cut Kids' Safety Scissors out of the drawer and handed them over. Other than Furious Gibbon and Uncle Barry yelling 'das Formular ist falsch', it was completely silent. I snipped a corner off the samosa. Nilesh gasped.

I then gently scored along the outside and lifted the flap away, exposing its tasty innards.

I held out my hand. 'Microscope.'

Nilesh passed me Uncle Barry's reading glasses. I cast them over the samosa and inspected the contents.

'There is definitely a presence of onion,' I said.

'That would explain why I'm crying,' said Nilesh.

I sifted through, looking for more clues.

'Pea,' I said.

'I could do with one,' said Nilesh.

I dipped a finger into the mix and licked it. 'Potato.'

Nilesh nodded, writing it all down.

'And finally,' I said, 'Carrot.'

We then set about finding the ingredients. The potatoes seemed to have shoots growing out of them, but I just dug them out. You see, Chuck, even though I have excellent business knowledge, I'm not much of a cook. Just last week, I got thrown out of my Food Tech class because I made too much noise piercing the film lid.

Nevertheless, we were determined to make the best samosas the world had ever seen. We started by chopping the veg into tiny pieces, just like Nilesh's nan did, and then putting them in a big pan with some water.

I turned the radio on so no one would get suspicious. It was on the classical station, which isn't normally my kind of thing, but then I remembered what you said and left it on.

CHUCK'S PEP TALK

Sometimes, when I'm stuck, I listen to classical music to get my brain going. My favourite composer is Wolfgang Awesomeadeus Mozart, but Beethoven is pretty Greathoven!

I nodded along with the radio and rubbed my chin like intellectuals do. Nilesh looked at me weirdly and asked for the zillionth time when we were going to play Epic Warfare. I ignored him and stirred the mix. It looked kind of disgusting and sick-like, but I knew it would taste great when it was done.

I set Nilesh to work making the samosa casing. He said he'd watched his nan do them a few times and thought it wouldn't be that hard.

Nine attempts later, he was nearly in tears.

'I thought you said you watched her!' I said.

'I did!' he replied. 'I just used to get bored and go and do something else.'

I sighed and looked at the discarded attempts on the side. Some were too thick, others too thin, most of them were completely the wrong shape.

Mum came in, changed the radio to that sports station where angry men phone up and scream about footballers, and asked what we were doing.

I said, 'We're making samosas for the competition tomorrow.'

Mum frowned, all confused. 'What, the tug of war?'

I exchanged a glance with Nilesh. 'No, we're not making samosas for a tug of war, we're making them for a cooking competition.'

Mum laughed and said, 'But you can't cook!'

'I'm learning,' I said. 'I'm trying to get mine and Nilesh's business up and running so we can move out of here.'

Mum sighed. 'Well, it's nice that you're trying

to help, I suppose. Look. I've got to cook dinner, so this will have to wait until later. Nilesh is more than welcome to stay, though.'

We headed upstairs and played Epic Warfare for a few hours. Nilesh was loving it, trying to devise new strategies to take down the  biggest players on the scene. He even gave us code names. He's Alpha and I'm Delta. When I complained, he told me he could always name me after my real initial in the military alphabet and call me Foxtrot and I shut up.

The trouble is, Chuck, I'm just not as into it any more. I mean, when you're part of the Complete Road to Awesomeness Program, you begin to see computer games for what they really are—a distraction. I think Nilesh could tell I'd lost some enthusiasm, because he kept moaning that we had no chance of beating last year's placing at the regional tournament.

Anyway, straight after dinner, Nilesh and I

went back to the kitchen to resume work on our samosas. It was seven o'clock. We had to be at Safebuy for ten the next morning. We had fifteen hours. Easy, right?

IT'S BUSINESS TIME

We were woken up by my dad walking in. In his pants. Nilesh was asleep on the floor and my head was resting in a bowl of flour.

'What's going on here?' Dad yelled.

I shot up, sending self-raising flying everywhere. 'What time is it?'

'Half seven. Why?'

I shook Nilesh. 'We've got to get to Safebuy!'

He groaned and rubbed his eyes. 'But we didn't manage to make the casing.'

'Then we'll just have to improvise,' I said, searching the cupboards. 'Ah, here we go.'

I snatched a bag of nachos, and before Dad could stop me, opened it and emptied them out onto the worktop.

Quickly, I grabbed the samosa filling out of the fridge, scooped some onto a nacho, then pressed another nacho on top, creating what kind of looked like a samosa if you squinted and had really bad eyesight anyway.

'But these aren't samosas,' said Nilesh.

'Th-they're a new thing,' I said. 'A hybrid. Indian meets Mexican. We could do a whole line of these things, chicken tikka burrito . . . um, enchillaji. We could call ourselves El Proppadum . . . o.'

'El Proppadumo?' said Dad. 'You're off your rocker.'

Luckily, I managed to convince Dad to put on some clothes and drive us over to the supermarket.

The other competitors were already there. They were mostly people we didn't know—except for one, Malvern Pope. I couldn't believe he was there. Actually, what am I saying? Of course I could. He treats EVERYTHING like a competition. And he's worse than ever now because last month he lost the town's junior film competition to a Year Seven called David Smythe.

Tammerstone Times

TWELVE YEARS A DAVE WINS BEST PICTURE.

When Malvern saw us, he grinned all smug-like. His Dad did too.

'Hey, Smallhouse,' said Malvern Sr. 'Fancy seeing you here. Not dressed as a tiger any more?'

Dad leaned down to me. 'Forget it, I'm not doing it.'

I glanced over at the registration table. A stand with the rules printed on it clearly stated that all under-eighteens had to be accompanied by an adult.

'Come on, Dad,' I said. 'This could be the start of something really cool! And we always used to do fun stuff like this.'

Dad blinked hard, then rubbed his bristly chin.
'OK, fine.'

CHUCK'S PEP TALK

Business is like golf. Sometimes it'll be rough. Sometimes
there'll be traps. But if you never lose sight of the green,
you can't lose.

Once we'd signed El Proppadumo up, we were
escorted to our table in the frozen food section.
Despite my protestations, we were put next to
the Popes and their Chocotastic Surprises. I placed
our Sombrerosas™ in an artistic arrangement.

Malvern Sr kept droning on to Dad about how
he'd been given his recipe by a Michelin-starred
chef he met on a work trip to Paris last month.
Then he asked if Dad got to go on many trips in
his new job. Dad said yes, because technically,
chasing an escaped Dobermann around a
butcher's shop could be considered a trip.

I looked around. There were twenty entrants,

each hoping that their treats would be declared the winner. The store PA crackled into life and the bloke from the desk said, 'Ladies and gentlemen, please welcome Dame Edith Tetchley.'

Everyone gasped. Yes, it was the real Dame Edith Tetchley, judge of the Big Cook Off. The most famous TV cooking expert ever, actually here in Tammerstone! She shuffled along the aisle, wearing a bright-pink trouser suit. She must be about ninety, but still looked super fierce.

She stopped at the first table and barked, 'What is this?'

The man struggled to get his words out. He was like a rabbit in the headlights, except instead of a car, it was a scary old lady who was really into cooking stuff.

Dame Edith bit into the cupcake like a snapping turtle. Her face screwed up, then she spat it into a tissue, then threw the tissue onto the plate, then threw the plate at a shop assistant.

'Disgusting,' she said, before moving on.

Fear swept along the line like an invisible Mexican wave. Nilesh mumbled something about needing a wee, but I held him in place.

She continued along the bank of tables, stopping at each one for a few seconds, and telling them how terrible their food was. She said to this one bloke, 'I wouldn't feed that to my DOG. Hang your head in SHAME.' Then, after she moved on, she looked back at him and yelled, 'I said HANG IT!'

Before long, Dame Edith was one table away from us. The Popes were next. Malvern Jr leaned over to me and whispered, 'Ready to see the winner crowned?'

Then he stood up straight, adjusted his dicky bow (yes, he was wearing a dicky bow) and gave Dame Edith a massive megawatt smile. She eyeballed him like she wanted to kick him in the gizzard. Then she picked up a chocolate brownie and took a tiny bite from the corner.

'It's triple chocolate,' said Malvern. 'Made with the finest—'

Dame Edith held up a wrinkly hand to silence him and took another bite. She chewed it for a few seconds, swallowed and fixed her cold blue eyes on Malvern's face.

'Awful,' she said. 'It tastes like death.'

Nilesh and I laughed so hard we missed Lady Edith glaring at us. 'And just what are you two guffawing at?'

'N-nothing, ma'am,' I said. 'We're just so happy to be here, that we couldn't help it.' Then I burst into laughter again. 'Tastes like death. Brilliant.'

Dame Edith grumbled something about firing her publicist and poked at our plate.

'What are these?' she asked.

'These are Sombrerosas™, ma'am,' I said. 'Mexican–Indian fusion.'

She raised an eyebrow. 'Well, it's different, I'll give you that.'

I snuck a quick glance at the Popes. From the expressions on their faces, you'd have thought they were witnessing a bus crash.

Dame Edith picked up a Sombrerosa™ and took a bite. I watched her face closely. She blinked hard a couple of times as she chewed. She seemed to be searching for the right words.

'This is . . .' she began.

We leaned forward. Everyone in the store was watching and waiting. This was going to be the first one she liked. I exchanged a look with Dad. Even he looked a bit excited. We were going to win the competition. A hundred grand in the bank!

'. . . the worst thing I have ever put in my mouth. That's it, I'm going home. The competition is cancelled.'

With that, she turned and stormed off, kicking over a pyramid of Rice Krispies boxes on her way out.

No one could believe it. The Sombrerosas™ had finished off the queen of food judgery. It's already made the news:

Tammerstone Times ONLINE

 | NEWS | SPORT | WHAT'S ON | ANNOUNCEMENTS | BUY & SELL | Q

DISGUSTING DELICACIES DON'T DELIGHT DAME

Tammerstone treats tasted terrible, Tetchley tells Times

On the way home, Nilesh turned to me and said, 'Have you finished trying to be Awesome yet?'

Before I could answer, Dad's phone rang. He grumbled and answered using speakerphone.

'What is it, Barry?'

'I am going to have to ask you to vacate the house tonight,' he said. 'I am taking new photographs of the house with my new state-of-the-art digital camera, which I hope will entice some buyers.'

'Fine,' said Dad. 'We're not stopping you.'

'No,' said Uncle Barry. 'I can't have you hanging around the house, making it look untidy.'

After Uncle Barry had hung up, Dad looked at us in the mirror. 'Looks like it's chippy tea tonight, Freddie. We'll eat it in the car.'

I nudged Nilesh. 'There's no way I've finished trying to be Awesome,' I said. 'In fact, I haven't even got started.'

CHUCK'S PEP TALK

Hey, Champ. If you ever need a pick-me-up, Chuck's got your back with his Motivational Acrostic Poem! Write it down and carry it around in your wallet, so you have it whenever you need it.

CHUCK'S MOTIVATIONAL ACROSTIC POEM

S — Success.

U — U can be successful.

C — C? I told you you could be successful.

C — C above.

E — Everybody knows you can be successful.

S — Success.

S — Success.

THE NEXT PHASE

OK, Chuck, so Sombrerosas™ didn't quite work out, but I'm not going to let it put me off. I have lots of different projects in the pipeline. I won't go into too much detail, but let's just say I'm looking at becoming a masked professional wrestler called El Frederico.

But I have some more immediate plans. After spending the day avoiding Malvern and his two massive goon mates, Lee Fields and Perry Crofts, because I knew he'd be in an awful mood and out for revenge, I went to Dad's work—the Police Dog Training Centre. I had the idea of talking to his boss, Mr Clinker, to see if he would give Dad the promotion he needed. He'd been going on about it for ages, and I thought I could convince him that Dad was the right man for the job.

CHUCK'S PEP TALK

If you want something, you got to get out there,
grab it by the scruff of its neck and say YOU ARE MINE.

WARNING: Do not try this with actual people.

I found Dad outside, applying a plaster to his
latest wound and writing 'padding needs to be
thicker' on a piece of paper.

'What are you doing here?' he said. 'I don't
have any money, so forget it.'

'I don't want money,' I said. 'I'm here to speak
to Mr Clinker.'

Dad stood upright and looked at me like
I'd suggested running through a safari park,
slathered in blood.

'Are you crazy? Why would you want to speak
to him?'

'To put in a word for you—get you that
promotion,' I said. 'He'll see me and take pity
on us.'

'One,' said Dad. 'I don't want pity, and two,
you need a heart to feel pity and that miserable

little trout Clinker doesn't have one. He has a shrivelled, blackened—'

'SMALLHOUSE!'

Dad jumped so high, he nearly whooshed over the chainlink fence. Mr Clinker rounded the corner. He's a weird-looking little man with three thick strands of hair plastered across his bald dome like bacon on a Christmas turkey.

'I'm not paying you to stand around talking to weird kids off the street, so get in that cage. We've got a new range of crotch protectors that need testing.'

'Th-this is my son, Mr Clinker,' said Dad.

Mr Clinker grunted. 'Oh really? Is this the Police Dog Training Centre or a crèche? Because if it's a crèche, I should probably clear out all the police dogs.'

'Hi Mr Clinker,' I said, giving him the most Awesome grin I could muster. 'It's actually you I wanted to speak to. I was wondering if you could give my dad a promotion.'

Mr Clinker's smirking face cracked into a huge grin and he started laughing. Really hard.

He sounded like an asthmatic penguin.

'Oh, that's a good one,' he panted, wiping tears from his eyes. 'Hey Smallhouse, you didn't tell me your kid was a comedian.'

Dad laughed a little bit, but I could tell he was faking it.

Mr Clinker walked over to me and crouched so his face was disgustingly close to my face. His breath smelled like a warm rubbish bin.

'I wouldn't promote your father if he had a printer in his bum that dispensed winning lottery tickets. He's useless.'

I glanced up at Dad, but he just stared at the floor.

'Tell you what,' said Clinker. 'The two of you can make yourselves useful and walk Mittens. He's a two person job.'

'What?' Dad cried. 'I can't have Freddie do that!'

Mr Clinker stepped closer to Dad and said, 'Do you want him to grow up to be a loser like his old man?'

'But Mr Clinker,' Dad sighed.

'But nothing,' said Clinker. 'If you disobey my orders, I will dock your pay, now bring him out.'

'Y-yes sir.'

Dad scurried away to a stable-like building and came out with the most enormous dog you've ever seen in your life, straining at the lead. I gulped.

'Um, Mr Clinker,' I said. 'Did you call him Mittens because he gives strong protection but is really quite sweet and fluffy?'

He said, 'No. It's because he likes to try and bite people's hands off.'

This time I gulped so hard I almost swallowed my own throat.

Clinker grabbed the lead and passed it to me. He said, 'Mittens knows two commands: heel and kill. Make sure you say them clearly because you do NOT want to get them mixed up.'

* * *

So me and Dad headed off with Mittens the psycho dog. We didn't speak much. I guess Dad was a bit embarrassed about the way Mr Clinker spoke to him in front of me. I totally understand why Dad spends most nights cursing Clinker's name to any god that might be listening. He's the worst.

Apart from that, the walk was OK. Mittens became more relaxed as we went on and after a while, Dad let me hold the lead.

We walked through the park, where every dog seemed to give Mittens a wide berth. We walked all the way around it, taking our time. Dad didn't seem to be in a hurry to get back to work.

When we left the park and got to the square by the church, there was a huge crowd, with loads of local news cameras. I stood on my tiptoes and saw that a war memorial parade was ending. Loads of really old blokes with medals were there. Now, they are truly Awesome, Chuck, so Dad and I stopped to pay our respects. Also, Dad needed a wee and there was a public toilet nearby.

'Will you be OK while I'm gone?' he asked.

By this time, Mittens was sitting down and relaxing.

'We'll be fine,' I said.

And we were. For about two minutes.

Just as the last old soldier was leaving the parade, a skinny bloke in a tracksuit ran up to him, ripped the medals off his chest and took off down the road. Some people tried to give chase, but he was too fast.

I looked down at Mittens. He looked back at me, steely determination in his eyes. We both knew what to do.

I unclipped the lead.

'KILL, MITTENS!'

'NO, NOT ME, THE ONE WHO'S RUNNING!'

The hellhound took off down the road, nearly knocking the old men over. The thief screamed and tried to run faster, but he was no match for Mittens, who soon had his skinny leg in his enormous mouth.

I ran after him and shouted 'heel' before he

could get around to ripping the thief's hands off. I grabbed the medals off the floor and gave them back to the old man. All the reporters from the march followed for photos and interviews. I was going to be famous—a real hero. An embodiment of Awesomeness. Maybe I could cash in and make personal appearances as the Tammerstone Hero. Dad could come on board and use his old business skills to sell my official merch. We'd be out of Uncle Barry's in no time at all! At the very least, it would guarantee Dad a promotion. We headed back to the centre to tell Mr Clinker what happened.

Clinker glared at me while I breathlessly told the story, squeezing a heavy-duty dog chew in his hand.

'So what you're saying is, Mittens saved an old man's medals?' he said.

I nodded, still on a high.

'And he did it by breaking free?'

'In a way,' I said.

Clinker nodded and threw the chew into a box. 'So what you're REALLY saying is, you're incompetent, Smallhouse.'

Dad's eyes went massive. 'N-n-no,' he babbled.

'I was actually holding the lead, Mr Clinker,' I said.

Clinker slowly stepped forward and squared up to Dad. 'And where were you?'

Dad cleared his throat. 'I was, um, indisposed, sir.'

'SPEAK ENGLISH, SMALLHOUSE,' Clinker barked.

'I was having a wee,' said Dad, looking like he was being deflated.

'And you really expect me to give you a promotion?' said Clinker. 'You're lucky I haven't fired you. Now get in that cage. Those crotch protectors aren't going to test themselves.'

And that's not the worst of it, Chuck. I got home and saw this:

DOG SAVES WAR VETERAN

I phoned up the paper and asked them why they cut me off the picture. They said the dog was more photogenic.

Back to square one, Chuck.

THE VIEWING

We've got a viewing, Chuck. The first viewing of Uncle Barry's house in over a month. Those photos he took with his fancy new camera must have worked. He's being cagey about the details—all he'd tell us is that they're a couple called the Turkletons.

Uncle Barry made us clean the house from top-to-bottom before they arrived. I didn't see why we had to help, because all we were doing was speeding up our own homelessness, but Uncle Barry was constantly cracking the whip. Well, not literally.

By the time we were finished, the place was gleaming. You could see your face in Uncle Barry's 'Most Fines Issued' plaques.

I tried to speak to Mum and Dad about it, but they wouldn't listen. Apparently, it's Uncle Barry's house and he can do what he likes with it.

Except let us have it. Apparently, that's out of the question.

In the end, I called Nilesh to brainstorm.

'You could fart loads,' he said over the banging sounds of Epic Warfare. 'They might think there's something wrong with the drains.'

'I can't just fart on demand,' I said.

'Shame,' said Nilesh. 'That would be cool. Aw come on, TankBoy661, don't be a noob all your life.'

I tutted. 'Can you stop the game for one second? This is important.'

Nilesh grumbled and I heard the sound of the game going off. 'Now come on, think,' I said. 'What is the worst thing you could find in a house?'

Nilesh went quiet, then clapped and said 'Dead bodies? I'd hate there to be dead bodies in my house.'

'Where am I going to get dead bodies at such short notice?' I said. Then I stopped. An idea began to formulate in my brain. An Awesome idea. 'But maybe we're on the right track.'

Nilesh gasped. 'If you think I'm digging up corpses in the cemetery, you can forget it.'

'I won't need you to do that,' I said. 'But I will need you to do something.'

'I was afraid of that,' said Nilesh.

CHUCK'S PEP TALK

When you're faced with a big problem, remember that YOU are bigger than IT. Unless the problem is an escaped rhino. That's definitely bigger than you.

A couple of hours later, Nilesh was in our cupboard under the stairs. I had sneaked him in while Uncle Barry was scrubbing the bath.

'Do you really think this is going to work?' he said.

'It can't fail,' I replied.

There was a knock at the front door. I quickly slammed the door shut. I knew it must have been the Turkletons. 'Uncle Barry,' I yelled up the stairs. 'Do you want me to get it?'

'No I do not,' he said as he clomped down. 'Please stay out of the way for the duration of the visit.'

Of course, Chuck, I had no intention of doing anything of the sort. Mum and Dad had gone out, but I insisted on staying. As soon as Uncle Barry opened the front door, I ran into the kitchen and grabbed the tablet from the side. I went straight to YouTube and loaded up a video that was just ten minutes of knocking and groaning noises, then I dropped the tablet into a cardboard box, piled a load of crisp bags on top and shoved it in the cupboard.

As soon as I'd shut the door, the Turkletons walked in, along with Uncle Barry. They were pretty old, maybe a little bit younger than my grandad, all white hair and kind faces. I felt kind of bad about what was going to happen, but I had to put my family first.

Mrs Turkleton said, 'Well, it looks lovely so far.' She had no idea what she was walking in to. Uncle Barry gave me the stinkeye as if to say, 'I told you to stay away', but he didn't say anything.

'As you can see, this is the kitchen area,' he droned. 'All components meet the relevant regulations and all electrical appliances have been

PAT tested within the past calendar year.'

'Hey, can you hear something?' said Mr Turkleton.

They stopped and listened. Sure enough, the sound of knocking and groaning was coming out of the cupboard. The colour seemed to drain from the couple's faces.

'I suspect it's next door's television,' said Uncle Barry, who then seemed to catch himself and say, 'which isn't usually so loud.'

'Oh,' said Mrs Turkleton. 'For a minute there, I thought you had a ghost!'

The couple started laughing and Uncle Barry grudgingly joined in. It's weird seeing him laugh, Chuck. He sounds like a defective robot.

'We don't have a ghost,' I said. 'The only people that live here are me, Uncle Barry, Mum, Dad and Percival.'

Uncle Barry's forced smile disappeared and he stared at me like he was going to turn me into a ghost.

'Who's Percival?' Mr Turkleton asked. 'Is he your brother?'

I shook my head.

'A pet?' said Mrs Turkleton.

I shook my head again.

'Is he a friend?'

'I'm not sure what he is,' I said. 'He just stands in the corner of my room at night, crying for his governess.'

'Enough of this,' Uncle Barry snapped. 'There is no Percival. The boy is talking nonsense. Now come along, please. We will proceed to the living room.'

The Turkletons went first, as I hoped they would. Uncle Barry followed and I brought up the rear.

'The living room is of an adequate size,' said Uncle Barry. 'The bulk of your living can be done in this room without much difficulty.'

I cleared my throat. That was the signal for Nilesh. Instantly, the TV flicked on and a shadowy figure appeared on the screen.

'What's that?' said Mrs Turkleton.

Uncle Barry fumbled with the TV and switched it off, but it came back straight away. Good old long-range universal Switchyswitch remote.

Nilesh and I had quickly made a video and burned it onto a DVD. All we had to do was take a ghostly image from Google and record a spooky voice over the top of it.

'Miss Pennywhistle told me not to play by the old well,' wailed the ghost/Nilesh. 'Why didn't I listen?'

The Turkletons's eyes went massive. For a second I was a bit worried one of them was going to have a heart attack.

'Is . . . is that Percival?' Mr Turkleton said.

I nodded, but Uncle Barry screamed, 'No! This is nothing but tomfoolery and chicanery.' Then, right on cue, all the power went out. Nilesh had flicked the trip switch in the cupboard under the stairs. Then it came back on, then off, then on, until everything in the room blinked and flashed.

Uncle Barry dragged them both out and slammed the living-room door. 'I apologize for that,' he said. 'Let me just find out what is happening.'

He started towards the cupboard but stopped

when Mrs Turkleton said, 'We'll take it.'

'WHAT?' me and Uncle Barry yelled at the same time. I began to think that I was the one being trolled.

'We are keen ghost hunters,' said Mr Turkleton. 'This is our dream house.'

'So much psychic energy,' Mrs Turkleton whispered, waving her fingers in the air.

'We'll have to talk money,' said Uncle Barry, seeming as bewildered as me.

'We'll pay the full asking price,' said Mr Turkleton. 'Gosh, I can't wait to bring the Paranormal Club to this place.'

So how about that, Chuck? Isn't that just my luck? I tried to scare away the biggest ghost freaks in Tammerstone. And get this: they said they wanted to move in as quickly as possible, so it looks like we'll only have a month before we're out on our ears. Uncle Barry was so happy, he even forgot to tell me off for my Percival stunt. What am I going to do now?

CHUCK'S PEP TALK

The thing about us Willards is that we never accept defeat—my dad didn't, his dad didn't, his dad, Baron Gustav von Willardenschultz kinda did, but we don't talk about him.

Point is, if you wanna be Awesome, you gotta learn to get back up when you're down. So here's what your old buddy Chuck wants you to do: Stand in front of a mirror right now and say to your reflection: **I AM AWESOME. I AM AWESOME. I AM AWESOME.**

MITTENS

I did what you said, Chuck, but then Uncle Barry came in and told me I was exceeding optimal noise levels for that time of the morning and would be subject to prosecution if I didn't immediately cease activity.

Mum and Dad have already started selling our stuff in preparation for us being homeless. Mum tried begging Uncle Barry to give us more time, but he wouldn't hear of it.

And it gets worse, Chuck. Get a load of this.

Tammerstone Times ONLINE

🏠 | NEWS | SPORT | WHAT'S ON | ANNOUNCEMENTS | BUY & SELL | 🔍

HERO DOG MITTENS GETS TV SHOW

Mittens, the courageous canine who took down a dastardly thief, has been rewarded for his heroics with a prime-time TV series.

The show, titled *Saturday Night with Mittens* will be a fun-packed hour of comedy and music hosted by the dog himself.

The town's MP said, 'It is wonderful news for Tammerstone. Finally our most famous resident isn't that man that can fart the alphabet.'

Saturday Night with Mittens is scheduled to be broadcast in the autumn.

That should be MY TV show. I mean, have you ever heard anything so ridiculous in your life? Mittens is just the dog, I was the one controlling him. It's like if they ignored Neil Armstrong and gave a medal to the rocket.

Then, tonight, when I got home from Nilesh's, I found Dad sitting at the kitchen table with his face buried in the tablecloth. Mum was rubbing his back.

'What's the matter?' I asked.

'It's your dad's job,' said Mum.

'What about it?'

Dad looked up from the table. He had a piece of alphabetti spaghetti stuck to his forehead. It was an L.

'Clinker sacked me,' he said.

'What?' I cried. 'Why?'

Dad sighed. 'Because he said it's my fault we've lost our best dog.'

'But he can't do that,' I said.

'Yes he can,' said Dad. 'My contract was one page long and all it included was a clause that I couldn't sue them if a dog ripped my face off.'

I couldn't believe what I was hearing, Chuck. We now only had one income. When Uncle Barry disappeared to Germany, we would have nothing.

'I'll help you get a new job,' I said. 'Come on, we'll go out now.'

Dad plonked his face back down on the table. 'The only thing I'm good for is the knacker's yard,' he said.

'What's that, some kind of pub?' I asked.

They didn't answer me, but I guessed it wasn't.

If Dad wasn't going to help get himself a job, it was going to have to be down to me.

CHUCK'S PEP TALK

Now you're a top entrepreneur, why not get involved in the stock market? Shares in Chuck Willard International are reasonably priced and will only go UP, UP, UP!*

So talk to your broker and climb aboard the Chuck Express to **AWESOMETOWN**, calling at **SUCCESSVILLE**, **DOLLARSDALE** and **PORT YOU'RE THE GREATEST**! MIND THE GAP!

* Not a guarantee.

THE JOB HUNT

By the time I got into town, a lot of the shops were closing and hardly any of them were interested in talking to me about job opportunities for my dad. In the end, only the manager of Griddler's Café would hear me out.

'What experience does he have?' she asked.

'He worked in insurance since, like, forever, then he ran his own antiques business and did some work with animals,' I said, cleverly not mentioning that the work with animals was actually being chewed by them.

The manager nodded, seeming impressed. 'Well, in that case, get him to give me a call. I've got a Saturday shift working in the kitchen become available.'

I thought that sounded great, but when I went home and told him, he didn't seem into it.

'I appreciate the effort, son, but I'd make more money on the dole,' he said.

'What's the dole?' I asked.

'It's money for nothing,' said Uncle Barry. 'A safety net for the lazy.'

'You'll be the one needing a safety net when I throw you out of the window,' said Dad.

'Brian,' Mum warned.

'May I remind you that you are guests in this house and I can legally evict you at any time,' said Uncle Barry.

And he'd do it, as well, Chuck. I had to go back to the drawing board. I went upstairs and googled local jobs. Much like the Griddler's one, there didn't seem to be anything that would be worth Dad's while. Maybe I had to think bigger. Something outside Tammerstone.

While I was searching for jobs, something caught my eye in the news column.

That was all I had to read, Chuck. I am going to make Dad famous.

NEWS

MITTENS LAUNCHES SEARCH FOR TALENT

Hero dog and all-round great lad Mittens is searching for acts for his new show, Saturday Night with Mittens.

THE FAME GAME

So I guess the business world ain't all it's cracked up to be. That's cool. Not everyone is cut out to be an entrepreneur. Some of the most **AWESOME** people in the world don't have one iota of business acumen. I'm talking scientists, philosophers, writers, those kinds of guys. Problem is, they don't have the cash or the chicks either, so why not do **SOMETHING DIFFERENT?**

INTRODUCING—
FAME FOR
FAME'S SAKE!

Reality TV and YouTube have seen to it that ordinary schlubs like you can become world famous. All you need is a little moxy and a pinch of Chuck Willard's patented Awesomeness. Here are my top three tips for making it in the Fame Game.

1 Look for opportunities. Literally everything is a chance to get your face out there. Something funny happen to you? Tell the story to your YouTube subscribers and watch your numbers grow. Eat a burrito that gave you the runs? Twitter needs to know about it. Witness a horrific car accident? Flip your cell to selfie mode and film yourself wailing and crying over the twisted wreckage. Everything can be exploited, my friend. Everything.

2 Get in with corporate sponsors by mentioning them in your videos and tweets whenever you can. Who knows? They might give you free stuff in return. Sounds pretty sweet, huh? As sweet as the sweet, sweet taste of Pepsi, I'll bet.

3 Send your headshots out to agents. They're a must if you want to make it in Hollywood. Try and pick some that show off all the different aspects of your personality. These are the ones I use. Luckily, every aspect of my personality is Awesome, so it was easy.
And that's all you need to know, my friend! Just promise you won't forget your old pal Chuck, when you're a superstar!

Imagine if Dad got a place on that show. Malvern Pope Sr would be sick as a pig. Junior, too. I could swan around school and nobody would mess with me because I had a famous dad. Of course, the tricky part was figuring out what he could do on there. To begin with I thought maybe he could show off his dog training skills with Mittens. Then I remembered that he never actually trained dogs, and that a Saturday night audience probably didn't want to watch a man being mauled.

I thought about his other talents. Yes, Dad did used to be keen on karaoke when we went on holiday, but then the man started pretending it was broken whenever he walked in. Obviously, he was good at antiques, too, but you can't really make entertainment out of that. Then I remembered something he really liked: practical jokes.

Dad was always pranking us before he went

sad. I remember another time we were on holiday, he hid under Mum's sunbed so he could reach from underneath and grab her. It would have been better if he hadn't accidentally got the wrong sunbed and grabbed a really big muscly man's wife, but the point is, it was a funny idea.

I thought about how it could work. Dad would prank members of the public while being secretly filmed. I bet Mittens's audience would love it.

I asked Dad if he was up for doing some pranks, so we could film them and send them to Mittens but he just said, 'I'm beginning to think my whole life is one big prank,' and turned away. Still, I wasn't ready to give up on the idea. If only there was a way I could do the pranks myself but have Dad take all the credit. Then I remembered the old suit of armour in the garage and a brilliant plan started to form in my mind.

Hold on to your hat, Chuck, because this might be the most Awesome idea I've ever come up with.

DETECTING AN OPPORTUNITY

'Are you sure this is a good idea?' Nilesh panted. 'What if you suffocate?'

'Stop yapping and throw more dirt on me,' I said. 'We don't have much time.'

I was lying in a shallow hole in the middle of Swinford Battlefield, wearing the suit of armour. You'd think being buried alive would freak me out, but I was so committed to the prank that it didn't bother me. Plus, I was only going to be covered in a couple of centimetres of soil, and I would breathe through a straw. It might have been better if it wasn't a novelty Mickey Mouse twisty straw, but it was the only one I could find.

We had hurried out to be here on time because I'd checked the Tammerstone Archaeological Society Facebook page and found out that they would be arriving at ten sharp and I had to be fully buried before then. Nilesh couldn't find his glasses, but I insisted there was no time for him to look for them. Every second was going to be vital.

Nilesh piled dirt on me with the spade, making sure there was no armour left on display. I tried to ignore the claustrophobic feelings swirling in my head and concentrate on how Awesome this was going to be.

'Hey, I think the archaeologists are coming,' said Nilesh, and I began to mentally prepare for what I was going to do. But then he said, 'Actually . . . no. No, that's just some bushes.'

Maybe I should have let him find his glasses after all.

'Wait,' he said. 'These are definitely archaeologists. They're moving and everything. I'm going to my hiding place.'

I hoped they were actual people and he hadn't just seen a pigeon and a plastic bag or something. Luckily, I heard voices in the distance so I knew he was right this time.

I closed my eyes and sucked on the twisty straw. This was going to be brilliant. When Mittens' crew saw this, they would beg Dad to join them. Then he'd be a rich megastar and we'd have our own house again.

The voices got louder. They were talking about looking for Medieval treasure. Perfect.

This bloke said, 'I'm going to check over by the fence. Florence, you concentrate on this area.'

I tried not to breathe too heavily, even though I was completely covered in metal and dirt and I was boiling. If they spotted me, it would be game over.

This Florence was close, I could hear her footsteps. She must have noticed the slightly disturbed earth because her pace quickened and soon she was right on me, her metal detector going crazy.

BEEP BEEP BEEP

I heard her gasp and say, 'I've got something.'

The beeping got quicker. She said. 'It's something big. Something really big.'

BEEP BEEP BEEP

'Oh my, it's not Medieval treasure, is it?'

BEEP BEEP BEEP

Here we go.

5 . . . 4 . . . 3 . . . 2 . . . 1

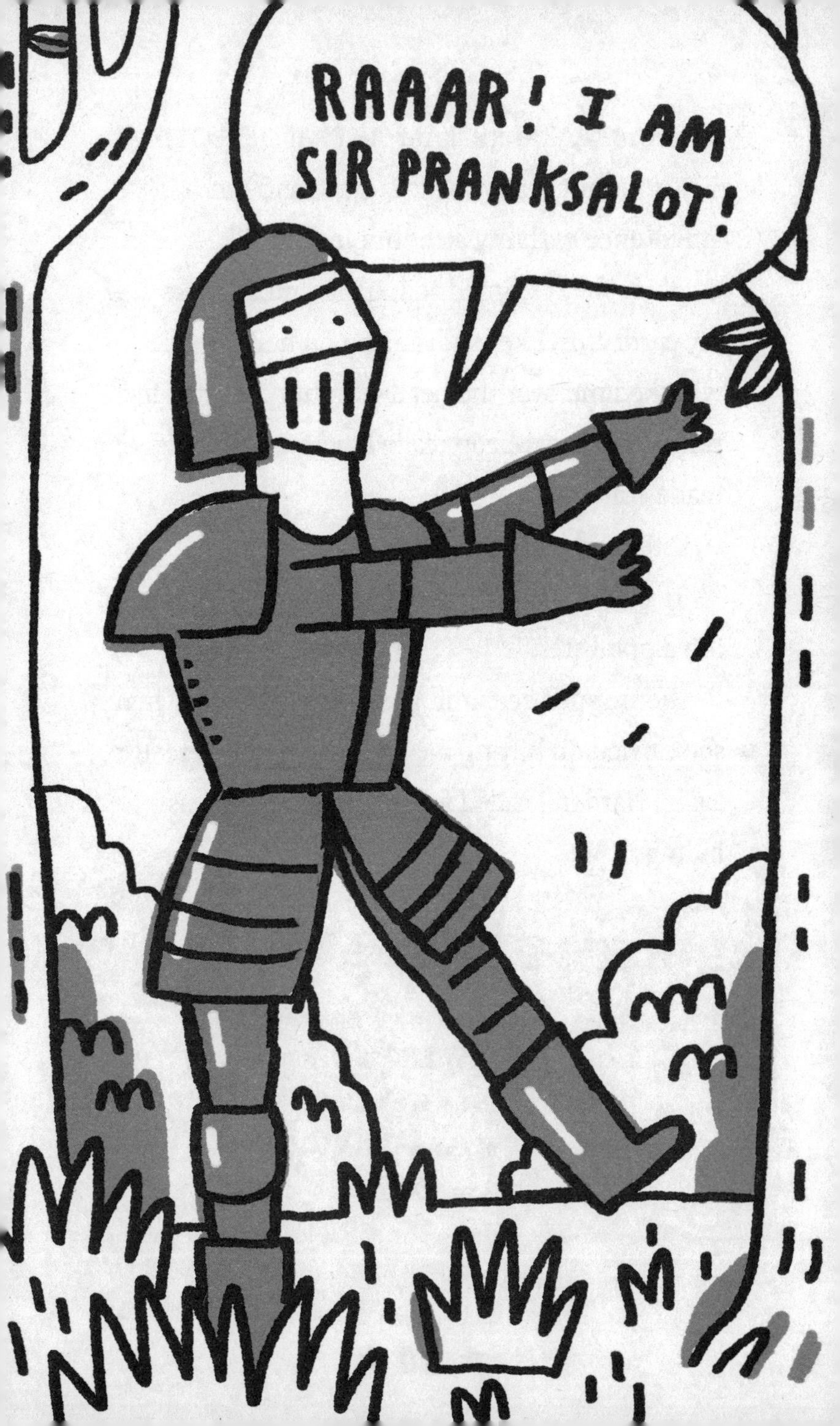
RAAAR! I AM SIR PRANKSALOT!

'RAAAAAARRRRR! I AM SIR PRANKSALOT!'

I leapt out of my shallow grave and ran at Florence with my arms out in front like a zombie. She screamed so loud it almost burst my eardrums. I kept advancing on her, but she whacked me over the head with her detector five times, making it beep really loud every time it made contact.

I stepped back and lifted my visor.

'It's OK,' I said. 'I'm not a real zombie knight. I'm a prankster!'

She stopped screaming and stared at me. Then she carried on hitting me with the metal detector again. Harder. I called for help but Nilesh was hiding.

CHUCK'S PEP TALK

When it feels like the whole world is against you, look within yourself to find the **AWESOME**. Place two fingers on your wrist, just below your palm. Feel that? That's your pulse. Now imagine that instead of **thud-THUD**, **thud-THUD**, it's going **awe-SOME**, **awe-SOME**.

NB. If you can feel **awe** and not **SOME**, call 911.

Eventually, I managed to clank away and take refuge in the Drive-Thru Maccies over the road. People were staring, but I didn't care. Even though I was nearly murdered to death by Florence and her band of angry archaeologists, I knew this would make a hell of a video.

After a few minutes, Nilesh joined me. I think he must have used the distraction of me being chased across the dual carriageway to slip by unnoticed.

'Come on then,' I said. 'Let's watch it back.'

He passed me his phone. It was confusing. There was a still image of my shallow knight grave, but nothing else.

'Where's the play button?' I asked Nilesh.

He took the phone off me and squinted at it. 'I can't see it,' he said. 'That's weird.'

I took it back and my heart sank. 'I can't believe it,' I yelled. 'You took a photo instead of a video!'

Nilesh frowned. 'Did I?'

'Yes,' I yelled, my voice barrelling off the inside of my helmet. 'How could you not just record a video?'

'Um, hello?' Nilesh said. 'You didn't let me get my glasses, remember? I couldn't see what I was doing.'

I facepalmed, or rather, helmetpalmed and it went quiet for a while.

'Do you want a McFlurry?' Nilesh asked.

CONFESSION

Yes, Chuck, another day, another attempt at digging my family out of its hole goes out the window.

I was so sure it would work, too. What could be funnier than a knight getting smacked about by a distressed amateur archaeologist? Of course, there's no way I can try it again now. They'll be expecting me. Plus, the helmet got a few dings in it from the metal detector. I was expecting Dad to go mad, but he just shrugged and said, 'I don't care. Let it rust, like everything else I care about.'

Later on, I went into the kitchen and found Uncle Barry on the phone,

'Yes, Mrs Turkleton, I look forward to it. Six o'clock tomorrow sounds perfect. Goodbye.'

He hung up and glared at me. 'Yes?'

'Mrs Turkleton?' I said, trying to remain all casual. 'What does she want? Has she decided she doesn't want to buy the house after all?'

'No,' Uncle Barry snapped.

'So what did she want?' I asked.

'Not that it is any of your business,' said Uncle Barry, 'but they are coming over to sign the paperwork that will finalize the sale of this house.'

I gasped. 'But that's happened really quickly.'

Uncle Barry chuckled to himself. 'It has, hasn't it?'

This can't be real, Chuck. I turned to the Awesomeness App for advice as I always do, and this is what you said:

CHUCK'S PEP TALK

Solutions to your problems can often be found in unexpected places. Keep those **AWESOME** eyes peeled!

I walked the streets looking in unexpected places (old phone boxes, in bushes, etc.) but came away empty-handed. In the end, there was only one place left to turn.

I knelt and clasped my hands together.

'Oh, Father,' I said. 'I need a miracle.'

'What is wrong, my child?' said the voice on

the other side of the screen.

'My family is about to be made homeless and I need some money to stop it. '

There was silence.

'Um, hello? '

'I don't know what kind of place you think this is, ' said the voice. 'But the church can't just give away money. '

'Why not? ' I said.

'We don't have it! ' said the voice.

'Come on! ' I moaned. 'All those gold statues out there must be worth a few quid. Can't you sell one? '

'. . . I'm going to have to ask you to leave, ' the voice said.

Great. Even God is against me.

'Wait a second,' I said. 'You're a priest, right?'

He sighed. 'Yes, why do you ask?'

I don't know what gave me the idea, Chuck. Maybe it was all the Awesomeness you'd taught me finally sparking in my brain, but in that moment, I came up with an idea that could save my family, or at the very least, buy us some time.

COMING SOON
to DOWNTOWN L.A.

THE FIRST EVER

Chuck Willard

RESTAURANT

FOR WHEN YOUR APPETITE CAN
ONLY BE SATED WITH AWESOME!

Hi, I'm *Chuck Willard*.

I'm so confident in the personally-selected dishes on the menu,
that if your meal is not completely **AWESOME**, you don't have
to pay!

For legal purposes, 'completely' means 'mostly' and 'Awesome' means 'edible'.

THE PLAN

I stood outside the house nervously checking my watch. He said he'd be here by now. If he didn't arrive before they signed the contract, it would all be a waste of time.

I ran around the back and checked that the kitchen door was open and that Uncle Barry wasn't in there. All clear. I could hear Uncle Barry and the Turkletons chatting in the lounge. Mr Turkleton was going on about how much he was looking forward to observing all the paranormal activity.

When I got back around the front, Father O'Flaherty was just pulling up in his holy Hyundai. I sprinted to greet him at the door.

'Thank you so much for this, Father,' I said. 'There's no time to waste, please come quickly.'

The old priest locked the car and grumbled under his breath. 'Very well,' he said. 'Show me where there have been the most disturbances.'

I led him around the back and into the kitchen.

'Mainly in here,' I said. 'Pots and pans banging. The fridge making weird noises. That kind of thing. Excuse me.'

I ducked out of the kitchen and into the lounge. The contracts lay on the coffee table and Mrs Turkleton was holding a pen.

'One moment,' I yelled.

Everyone stopped and looked at me. 'You should all come and see this,' I said. 'It may affect your decision.'

'Frederick,' Uncle Barry snapped. 'What is the meaning of this?'

I ignored him and led the Turkletons into the kitchen, where Father O'Flaherty was sprinkling holy water around and muttering prayers.

'What's happening?' Mr Turkleton cried, with a look on his face like he was watching a bridge fall down.

'I am cleansing this house of evil spirits!' Father O'Flaherty said.

'No!' Mrs Turkleton screamed. 'We love the evil spirits!'

'Stop this immediately,' Uncle Barry cried, but Father O'Flaherty wouldn't let anyone interfere with his heavenly mission and doused the kitchen with even greater urgency. Uncle Barry tried to wrestle the container out of his hands, but the old priest was stronger than he looked and yanked it away.

'You must be possessed, too,' Father O'Flaherty boomed. 'The power of Christ compels you!' And with that, he threw the rest of the water right in Uncle Barry's face.

'This house is now free,' said Father O'Flaherty. 'My invoice will be in the post.' And then he left.

'I can't believe it,' said Mr Turkleton. 'We can't buy this house now!'

YESSSSS!!!

Uncle Barry desperately tried to wipe the water off his face and go after the Turkletons. 'Please,' he said. 'This is all just a silly prank by my ingrate nephew. The house is still haunted.'

The Turkletons stopped. 'Prove it,' said Mrs Turkleton.

Uncle Barry flapped around as if he was

hoping the answer would be hiding in the walls somewhere. 'Go and check in the lounge,' he said. 'The priest didn't exorcise that.'

The Turkletons did as they were told and Uncle Barry marched up to me and jabbed his finger in my face. 'That was a low trick, Frederick, but it will not work.'

Then he stomped over to the tablet and tapped it a few times. 'You are not the only one who can partake in subterfuge,' he said, then placed it under the cutlery compartment in the top drawer.

'Wait a second, what are you doing?' I said.

Uncle Barry ignored me and went back into the lounge to fetch the Turkletons.

'Come back in here,' he said. 'The priest must have missed one.'

The groans and wails started up from the drawer.

Mr and Mrs Turkleton grinned at each other as if they'd just won the lottery.

'No way!' I cried. 'That isn't a ghost, it's just YouTube!'

'No, it's definitely real,' said Mr Turkleton, pulling a little black box out of his pocket. 'My spirit energy detector is going crazy!'

I looked at the box. I'm pretty sure it was a calculator.

'Yes, I can feel it,' said Mrs Turkleton. 'Whatever resides here is too powerful even for the Church! Let's get those contracts signed.'

CHUCK'S PEP TALK

See that? Doesn't look like much, does it? Put enough of them together, though and you've got yourself a mansion. Think about it.

THE NEW PLAN

The clock is ticking, Chuck. As soon as the Turkletons sort out their house sale, we are out of here. I have to find Dad a super-well-paid job and fast. Only something truly Awesome will suffice. The problem is, we've already ruled out reality TV star and musician, so the next thing to try is athlete.

Back when Dad was normal, he was always playing football and going on about how he had the 'Smallhouse killer instinct' and would have been a superstar if it wasn't for his dodgy knees. Problem is, even if I could somehow sort out his knees, he wouldn't even want to get out of bed. So it's down to me. Here's my six point plan for sporting Awesomeness.

1   Get really good at football.
2   Get signed by Tammerstone FC.
3   Become the best player.

4   Get signed by a top club.
5   Take Dad on as my agent/manager.
6   Become millionaires and live in a posh
    mansion somewhere exciting like Milan or
    Barcelona or Coventry.

Now, I've never been great at PE. In fact, you
might say I once managed to throw a discus at
my own head, but now I'm part of the Complete
Road to Awesomeness Program, I'm pretty sure I
can become great.

I watched your video on sports psychology, and
then later on at school, an opportunity dropped
into my lap that was too good to pass up.

Our PE teacher, Mr Gittins, was taking our
assembly because our headteacher Mr Bümfacé
was away. Wait, I should probably explain
his name, Chuck. It's actually pronounced
'Boomfachay' and if you say it any other way, you
get a detention. To be honest, I have no idea why
he decided to go into teaching.

Where was I? Oh yeah, Mr Gittins. He was
talking about how PE is the most important

subject because when your boat sinks, you can't algebra yourself to safety. Anyway, at the end, he said, 'The Year Eight football team is way down for Wednesday night's game against Woodlet. If we can't find one more substitute, we'll have to forfeit the game. Any volunteers?'

Every hand stayed down. No one wanted to play against Woodlet. They're the most brutal team in Tammerstone. Last time we played them, half our team got injured and the other half got Post Traumatic Stress Disorder.

Which is why even I was surprised to see my hand in the air.

'Freddie Smallhouse?' Mr Gittins cried. 'Are you serious?'

Everyone started laughing. Nilesh nudged me and gave me a 'what the hell are you doing' look.

I didn't care. I was doing what I had to do to preserve the dignity of my school. I mean, I wasn't about to see us give up without even trying. That would be the very opposite of Awesome.

'Do I really have no other volunteers?' Gittins asked.

When no other hands went up, he sighed and said, 'Fine. Hopefully we won't have to use you. It's after school on Wednesday.'

That gave me less than two days to somehow get good at football. I decided that I should start by learning some theory. At lunch, I headed to the computer lab and watched the first half of a Premier League football match on the internet. Here are the things I learned.

1 When the ref rules against you, always argue with him. It won't make a difference, but if you don't do it, you'll look weak.

2 When you get tackled, it's important to roll around on the floor as if you've had your knees blasted off by a bazooka. This might encourage the ref to rule against your opponent.

3 When you score, it is perfectly acceptable to rip your shirt off and passionately kiss your teammates. Doing this at any other time is a no-no.

I was watching another game after school. This one was Brazilian. It was pretty much the same as the one I watched earlier except whenever someone scored, the commentator would shout 'Goooooooooooal' and hold it for about ten minutes. After a while, Dad came in. He'd been job-hunting and I could tell from his face it hadn't gone well.

'Hang on a minute,' he said, plonking himself down in a chair. 'Since when do you watch football?'

I shrugged and squinted at the screen. It was half-time and a giant pineapple was salsa dancing across the halfway line. 'Got a game tomorrow,' I said.

Dad sat up. 'A game?' he said. 'You mean like a computer game?'

I shook my head. The pineapple was twerking at this point.

'Table football?' he said.

'No,' I said. 'An actual game.'

Dad looked at me as if I'd told him I was changing my name to Mrs Bumblebee and joining the circus as a bearded lady. 'But you can't play football.'

'Thanks for the vote of confidence,' I said.

'I didn't mean it like that,' said Dad. 'I'm just surprised, that's all. I mean, you didn't inherit the Smallhouse killer instinct, did you? You're more like your mother or your Uncle Barry.'

I glanced outside and saw Uncle Barry measuring the lawn with a ruler to check that it wasn't exceeding regulations. Yes, he has regulations for grass.

'Ah cheers,' I said.

Dad stood up. Slowly, on account of his dodgy knees. 'Come on,' he said. 'Let's go down the park before it gets dark. To quote my old coach, Jimmy Stack, 'You can't teach anyone to be great at football, but you can teach them to be good.'

CHUCK'S PEP TALK

If you're striving for excellence in the world of athletics, you need your own set of Chuck Willard Weights!

Not only are they crafted from the finest materials, but they talk to you with every rep!

And they start at just $89.95, so breaking a sweat won't break the bank!

EXPECTATION VS REALITY

Dad sat cross-legged on the penalty spot with his head in his hands.

'Not good?' I asked.

Dad didn't answer. His horrified silence said more than words ever could.

I mean, it started off OK, Chuck. Dad got me to do some stretches and I nailed that. I was stretching like there was no tomorrow. It's just the football bit that was the problem. Breaking it down, the main issue was Expectation vs Reality.

EXPECTATION	REALITY
Dad expected me to dribble the ball.	I fell over the ball.
Dad expected me to pass the ball to him.	I passed the ball to an old man walking a dog.

| Dad expected me to score a goal. | I banana-d the ball into a garden and smashed a greenhouse and we had to run away quite fast. |

And so on.

Dad said I should drop out of the team, but there's no way that could happen. I know that once I get out there on the pitch, I will rise to the occasion.

Nevertheless, as soon as we got home, I got straight on the tablet and logged on to the Complete Road to Awesomeness Program. I knew there would be something on there that would help me.

SPORTS

So you wanna be a big time athlete, huh? You look at those magnificent specimens on your TV, winning trophies, medals, and hot chicks, and you want a piece of that action, don't you?

Well, what you may not realize is that behind every successful sports star is years of dedication and hard work, and obsessive attention to detail as they hone their craft. Now, Chuck can't do that for you, but what he can do is instil in you a winning mentality.

Introducing the **CHUCK WILLARD AWESOME SPORTS HYPNOSIS PLAN**. Listening to just one of my top notch audio experiences while you hunker down for the night will give you the grounding you need in the sport of your choice.

You know record-breaking Olympic swimmer, Michael Phelps? Well, he swears by* my hypnosis**! So why don't you become a winner like him and check it out?

* at
** me whenever I contact him.

There's nothing like the buzz of a locker room before a big game. The other lads were full of 'bantz'—'They're the skinniest legs I've seen since I visited the flamingo enclosure at the zoo.' 'You stink worse than an explosion in a BO factory.' And the old classic, 'What are you doing here, Smallhouse? You can't play football to save your life.' Classic footballing camaraderie.

Little did my teammates know, last night I had paid the very reasonable price of £8.99 to immerse myself in the Awesomeness of your Awesome Sports Hypnosis Plan and would likely be playing football better than any of them.

When I woke up this morning, I truly felt like a different person. Before, whenever I saw people like Tom "best in the world at every sport ever invented" Wilkie strut around, I would struggle to even consider myself the same species as him. Now, I am his equal. I felt confident and accomplished and poised. I felt like a real football star.

Now, I knew I wasn't going to get a chance to prove it straight away. In fact, Mr Gittins straight up told me that of the three substitutes, I was third choice, and the other two were Regis Skitchley who has permanent nosebleeds, and Hans Schmolschmeier, the Austrian exchange student who has one leg shorter than the other. Still, I was excited just to be part of it.

The atmosphere was charged as we made our way to the field. Woodlet are a notoriously tough team. Apparently they picked up eighteen red cards in their last tournament.

'Hey, monkey boy,' Malvern Pope hissed at me. 'Carry my water bottle.'

He threw a metal flask covered in purple velvet at me.

'But I'm a substitute, not a slave,' I protested.

I looked to my fellow subs for moral support but they didn't answer on account of the language barrier/nose leaking like a rusty bucket.

'That's where you're wrong, my idiotic friend,'

said Malvern. 'Because if you don't do everything I say, I will have you kicked off the team. Forever.'

'He will, you know,' said Chris McCluskey from 8C. 'When Mr Gittins tried to play him in midfield instead of up front, he got his dad's lawyer to threaten him.'

I carried the flask.

We found Woodlet already on the pitch, ready to go. I gulped. They really did look like a hard bunch. And their teacher was terrifying too. He looked like the kind of man you see on TV at Christmas, chucking boulders and dragging tractors.

The starting eleven took their places on the pitch, while I stood on the side with Regis and Hans, holding Malvern's fancy flask. Nilesh said he couldn't make it because he had a dentist's appointment, but I had my suspicions about that excuse. The only crowd we had was Malvern Pope Sr, sitting on a deckchair with a glass of champagne and a cheese board.

Mr Gittins blew the whistle to kick off the match. The arrangement was, he would referee the first half, and the Woodlet teacher would ref the second.

As soon as the ball started zipping around, I felt an exhilarating sensation buzz through my insides. I just knew it was the Awesomeness from your hypnosis file awakening within me. Unfortunately, I didn't have anything to do with it. The team were doing perfectly well without having to resort to substitutes. Mr Gittins was keeping Woodlet in check, and Malvern had won a penalty by leaping through the air and rolling around on the floor like he was on fire. Then he hopped back up and scored as if nothing had happened.

Just before half-time, Woodlet scored, leading Malvern to scream at the defenders, the goalkeeper, and even the ball itself. When Mr Gittins blew for the end of the first half, Malvern turned to me and yelled, 'Hey, moron, where's my water?' I threw it to him and inwardly told myself off for not gobbing in it.

He even took over the team talk from Mr Gittins. I could tell he wanted to say something but then realized Malvern Sr could have been listening and didn't need the court case. Anyway, Chuck, Malvern's team talk was basically 'You're all useless and I'd be better off playing them by myself.' He'd obviously not watched any of your leadership seminars like I have, because all it did was make Henry Parks say 'Fine, you do that' and walk away. When it became clear that he definitely wasn't coming back, Mr Gittins replaced him with Hans. He said the midfield could do with some German efficiency. When Hans pointed out he was actually Austrian, he went a bit quiet and kicked a dribbling cone.

The second half was like a different game. Woodlet started hoofing us left, right, and centre and their teacher just let them get away with it. I asked Mr Gittins if he could do anything, but he said that the other teacher had already given him a wedgie around the back of the equipment cupboard and he'd be damned if that was going to happen again.

I decided to go for a jog around the pitch. If they needed me, I would have to be warmed up.

Plus, Regis going on about how much he poos if he ever eats gluten was kind of killing my buzz.

I got behind the goal and watched from there. Our boys were staggering around, bruised and aching thanks to Woodlet's brutal onslaught. Our right back got clattered by three of their players at once, so Regis had to replace him. Only Malvern managed to remain unscathed because every time one of Woodlet's players approached him, he belted the ball away as quickly as he could.

Tom Wilkie, our real star striker had the ball and was bearing down on goal. He only had the keeper to beat and would definitely score. Then the biggest, most ape-like Woodlet player sprinted across and took his legs out from under him, sending him spinning across the pitch like a broken Frisbee. Unlike Malvern, he didn't roll around screaming. He stayed still, biting his lip.

Mr Gittins went over to him and shook his head.

'It's no good,' he yelled at me. 'He's going to have to come off. Freddie, you're on.'

My stomach fluttered, my heart raced, my mouth dried up like a salty slug. This is it, I thought. My big moment. Time for Chuck's Awesomeness to shine.

'Good luck, son.'

I turned around and there was Dad, in the same grubby tracksuit he wore to train me at the rec.

'Wow, you actually came,' I said.

He nodded. 'I couldn't let you do it alone.'

Dad glanced over at Malvern Sr, who raised a glass to him. Dad quickly averted his eyes. 'Just try to stay out of the way of the ball and you'll be fine,' he said.

He was going to be amazed when he saw how good your hypnosis had made me, Chuck. He would think I'd been possessed by some kind of football demon.

'Freddie,' Mr Gittins yelled. 'Get on there!'

I jogged onto the pitch and took up position, up front next to Malvern. Malvern scowled at me, then whistled at Hans. 'Hey, Hansel,' he said. 'You're striker now. Smallhouse can get into defence, as far away from me as possible.' Hans and I did as we were told and I stood next to Louis Johnson at the back.

I expected to be nervous, but I really wasn't, Chuck. I knew the knowledge you had given me was lying in my brain, just waiting to be activated.

For a couple of minutes, I didn't have to do anything. The ball pinged around in the middle of the field and our players had to do their best to jump over all the vicious tackles and kicks. A Woodlet player belted the ball towards a teammate, but it bounced off Rich Monson's leg and whooshed into the air. It looped high, then came back down, right towards my head. I didn't know what to do. Your hypnotic advice wasn't kicking in. Maybe it was too soon. Maybe it wasn't working. I didn't have time to think of a third option, maybe because the ball had smacked off my head and whooshed back into the air, eventually landing at the feet of Conor Simpson.

'Nice header, son!' Dad yelled, as Conor jinked around a Woodlet player and tucked the ball into the back of the net. 2-1!

I couldn't believe it, Chuck. We were winning, and it was all down to my assist. I mean, yes, all I'd done was get hit in the skull by a ball, but as you say, 'It ain't the method, it's the result.'

Our joy was short-lived, though, when Woodlet hoofed the ball up the field, catching our goalie unawares because he was too busy having an argument with his girlfriend. By the time he'd seen the ball, it was already rolling over the line. 2-2. My Awesome Assist cancelled out.

There was only five minutes left, with it all to play for. Whoever won would have bragging rights for a whole year. Imagine being part of the first successful Lowes Park team in a decade. I'd be a hero!

As soon as we kicked off, Malvern took up his usual position near the Woodlet goal, leaving Hans to get smashed by three players at once. One of their hugest players started lumbering forward, repelling attempted tackles like a rhino shaking off gnats. Before he could get to me, he passed the ball to a quicker, smaller boy, who zigzagged around all the midfielders and defenders until it was just me between him and the goalkeeper.

I glanced over to the touchline. I saw Dad, willing me to tackle him and get the ball. I saw Malvern Sr laughing as if to say 'there's no way this loser can stop him'. I had to do it. I had to prove him wrong and make Dad proud. Luckily, your hypnotic programming kicked in immediately. I knew exactly what to do. I was ready. I was a superstar. I was Awesome.

The Woodlet player dribbled closer to me and I leapt forward, tackling him to the floor, shoulder first. Then I stood up, picked up the ball and ran to the other end of the pitch, where I spiked it and did a victory dance while yelling, 'TOUCHDOWN!'

I looked around, expecting everyone to be cheering, my team mates to be lifting me up and kissing me all over my head, my dad wiping away a tear and mouthing, 'I'm proud of you, son.' What actually happened was silence. Everyone was staring at me as if I had just beamed down from planet Wackadoodle. That was when some of your Awesomeness lifted—enough to allow me a peek into the real world. Your hypnosis had worked a treat. But it turns out that football in America and football in Britain are two very different things. I am now an expert quarterback, which is of zero use in Tammerstone, England.

Woodlet's teacher ran over, shoved a red card in my face and screamed, 'You're off for handball! Penalty to Woodlet!'

I trudged off the field, my head down, too embarrassed to look anyone in the eye, least of all Malvern, who was yelling, 'Can't you do ANYTHING right, you MORON?'

I heard Woodlet cheering as their penalty went in, then cheering again when their teacher blew the whistle for full-time.

Dad clapped his hand on my shoulder. 'Son,' he said.

'Yes, Dad?'

He sighed. 'What the hell was that?'

I was about to explain when Malvern Sr came over, shaking his head. 'I haven't seen anything that ridiculous on a football pitch since you played in that charity match back at MorganKemptonSchneffleberger.'

Dad gritted his teeth and said, 'I scored two goals in that game, Malvern, you know I did.'

Malvern Sr wasn't listening, though. 'Anyway, I trust your boy won't be involved in any further games.'

Dad went to argue, then seemed to remember that I had just literally scored a touchdown and probably thought better of it.

'Don't worry, Freddie,' said Malvern Sr. 'It can take us a while to figure out what we're good at. I mean, just look at your old Dad—he still hasn't. Catch you later, Smallhouses!'

On the way home, we stopped off at Safebuy and Dad had a row with the self-service checkout.

CHUCK'S PEP TALK

If you're ever feeling despondent, remember to keep your eye on the long game. Do you know where I'm writing this? In the hot tub on my million dollar yacht. It could be you sitting here one day.

P.S. I meant your own yacht. Stay away from the *SS Awesome*.

HAPPY BIRTHDAY

'No way,' Dad mumbled into the sofa pillow. 'Why would I want to celebrate forty-two years of mediocrity and failure?'

Mum winced. 'You're actually forty-three, sweetheart.'

Dad groaned and pushed the pillow into his face. 'Can't you leave me to my mid-life crisis in peace?'

Mum and I were standing over him with a birthday cake we had made together. The candles were close to burning out.

'Actually,' Uncle Barry called from the kitchen, where he was polishing his shoes, 'According to Tammerstone Council statistics, the average life expectancy for a male is 73.6 years, which means you passed the middle of your life some six years ago.'

Dad sat up. 'I'm going to bed.'

I can't help but feel like this is all my fault,

Chuck. All of my efforts to cheer Dad up have only made him worse. Like last night, Mum and I made him his favourite meal and put on his favourite old movie.

It was even worse for him because he was trying to find a new job. I mean, really trying, but he got nothing. He even tried out as a children's party entertainer.

Because of that I really wasn't in the mood for school this morning. Plus, literally everyone knew about what happened at the football match. That's how quick Malvern's web of gossip works. Somehow it had been exaggerated too, so now, I scored a touchdown, then stripped to my undercrackers and did ten laps of the field.

@LOWESPARKBANTZ Look at this idiot. Sign our petition to have him banned from sports for life.

'See, this is what happens when our kind get involved in sports,' Nilesh said to me at lunch. 'No good can come of it. The only competitive activities we're cut out for are gaming and *Star Wars* trivia quizzes.'

I sighed. 'I suppose you're right, Nilesh,' I said. 'I just wish I could help my dad get a job. A great one. It'd save our family and would really shut the Malverns up.'

Nilesh wrinkled his nose as he shovelled another load of chilli into his mouth. 'Ignore them,' he chombled. 'Getting back at Malvern won't make your life any better. Just concentrate on doing your own thing. By the way, the Epic Warfare regional tournament is fast approaching, so we need to get practising.'

He went on a bit after that, but I wasn't really listening, Chuck. I was distracted by Mr Bümfacé pinning a big poster to the wall.

LOWES PARK ELECTION

COULD YOU BE OUR FIRST SCHOOL PRESIDENT?

SUBMIT YOUR MANIFESTO BEFORE

FRIDAY 20TH MARCH.

THE BEST CANDIDATES WILL STAND IN AN ELECTION.

SEE MR BÜMFACE FOR MORE DETAILS.

'Wait, what are you looking at?' said Nilesh, turning around to read it himself. When he looked back at me, his eyes were massive.

'No,' he said. 'Don't even think about it.'

Too late, Chuck, I've already thought about it.

PUBLIC SERVICE

So you wanna go into politics, huh? Well, as a natural leader, your old pal Chuck has got you covered. Just check out this testimonial from someone who became an elected official after graduating from my **COMPLETE ROAD TO AWESOMENESS PROGRAM**.

> **"** *Chuck Willard helped me become the man I am today. Thanks to his invaluable advice, I was elected Governor of Wisconsin, and as soon as I get out of prison, I intend to run again.* **"**

So what are you waiting for? Get out there and make a difference! Mould your community in your own (and by extension, my) **AWESOME** image.

Here are my top three tips to help put your handsome face on the side of Mount Rushmore.

CHUCK'S AWESOME HINTS FOR AN AWESOME CAREER IN POLITICS

1 Tell people what they want to hear. Has your significant other ever asked if they looked fat and you've said 'no' even though you almost mistook them for a buffalo? You gotta do that but on a grand scale. Phrases like 'This is the greatest country/town in the world', 'We have a bright future' and 'That green smog is totally harmless' will be your friend.

2 Promise them the world. Seriously. Whatever they want, say you'll give it to them. If you win and can't do it, just deny you ever said it. Works every time.

3 You might feel **AWESOME**, but voters ain't gonna know it unless you show it. So eyes and teeth at all times. As big as possible. I've included a photo of myself to give you something to aim for.

Best of luck, and remember my patented slogan that I made up all by myself—'With great power comes great responsibility.'

The **AWESOMENESS** Party Manifesto

Members
Leader: Freddie Smallhouse
Deputy Leader: Nilesh Biswas

Awesome Party Pledges

→ An actual library. It has been locked up since last year and the populace of Lowes Park have no access to books. Not that there were that many in there, but you know what I mean.

→ A full check of all teaching staff's qualifications. We have some serious doubts about their credentials, especially that History teacher who always wears a cowboy hat and insists that everyone calls him 'Buffalo Bill'.

→ Private shower cubicles. I don't want to have to look at Garrett Thompson's spotty bum every week, thank you very much.

→ Drinking water that doesn't have bits in it.

→ Rehabilitate the school's image in the media. When you google Lowes Park High,

the top phrases you see are 'health hazard',
'embarrassment' and 'idiot farm'. This has to
stop.

The **AWESOMENESS** Party is the only party
that has your best interests at heart. If you vote
for Freddie Smallhouse as your president, you will
elect a leader who lives by the principles of life guru
Chuck Willard, and wants to make Lowes Park an
AWESOME place to get your education.

Remember: A vote for Freddie is a vote for
AWESOMENESS.

POLITICS

Thinking about it, Chuck, politics is perfect—forget business and TV stardom. With politics, you get to be Awesome, and you get to help people.

Helping people is a nice thing to do and it makes you feel good. One of my earliest memories is finding a coin on the floor and dropping it into a homeless man's cup, and the warm, fuzzy feeling it gave me has stayed with me ever since. The fact that the cup was full of tea and the man turned out not to be homeless doesn't matter. I was trying to make a difference.

When I showed my manifesto to Nilesh this morning, he went quiet for a bit. Then he said, 'I have one question.'

'Shoot,' I said, trying to sound all cool and president-like.

'Why?' he said.

I waited for the rest of the question, but it

seemed like that was it.

'Well,' I said. 'If I win, I can get my dad a job at the school, and we'll be sorted.'

Nilesh frowned. 'What kind of job?'

'I don't know,' I said. 'A teacher of some kind.'

'But don't you have to have qualifications to be a teacher?'

As soon as he said it, Mrs Timmins the Biology teacher/dinner lady walked past.

'All right, fair point,' said Nilesh. 'But who says school president is going to have that much say?'

I stopped and thought about it. 'There's never been one before, has there?' I said. 'That means I can make it what I want it to be. I'm learning Awesome communication skills from Chuck Willard all the time and I know I'll be able to use them to convince Mr Bümfacé to give Dad a job.'

Nilesh sighed a bit and nodded. I know he's still not a massive fan of yours, Chuck, but I'm sure he'll come around soon.

'And what would I have to do as Deputy Leader?' he said.

'It's very simple, Nilesh, ' I said. 'You would fill

in for me in the event that I am called away to an important summit, or I'm assassinated, or I don't know, I've got the dentist. You will also assist me in decision-making and have a say in policy matters.'

'Really?' he said.

'Of course.'

'Then can we make it a policy to spend at least a little bit of time practising for the tournament? We're going to be rusty if we don't start soon.'

I sighed. Epic Warfare is no longer a priority for me, but I need Nilesh on my team and this is the only way of getting him onside.

'Fine,' I said. 'We'll make time.'

'OK, I'm in,' said Nilesh. 'Don't make me regret it.'

At break, I headed to Mr Bümfacé's office with my application.

'You're standing in the election?' he asked.

I said, 'Yes, sir.'

He stared at me like I was mad. 'You? Freddie Smallhouse?'

'Yes sir,' I said. 'I believe I would be an . . .

Awesome candidate.'

Mr Bümfacé gawked at me for a bit then said, 'Well, I suppose it won't hurt to have some competition. The bookies' favourite is Malvern Pope and I think he'll take some beating.'

I wish he would take some beating, I thought.

'Well, I'm ready for the challenge,' I said. 'So what's the next step?'

Mr Bümfacé squinted at a piece of paper. 'There will be a hustings on Monday, where all the candidates will make a speech in front of the student council. The two who receive the most votes will go into the election.'

OK, Chuck, I need to write an amazing speech that will win over the student council. Do you have any tips for me?

CHUCK'S PEP TALK

Studies have shown that public speaking is the number one fear among the population, but it needn't be so. When you're up there, don't be scared of the audience—they should be scared of you! Feel the Awesomeness within come whooshing out of your windpipe, past your tonsils and out of your mouth.

Imagine your words filling the air like fireworks. *BOOM!* A Rocket. *Whoosh!* A Catherine Wheel. *Blammo!* Some other kind of firework.

Light up the sky, buddy, light up the sky.

ELECTION CANDIDATE SPEECHES

PRAWN MCKENZIE—THE *STAR WARS* PARTY

Vote for me, you should.

CHARLIE HACKENSACK—THE NUDIST PARTY

They say when you give a speech, you should imagine the audience naked. If I had it my way, I wouldn't have to.

HENRIETTA SMYTHE —THE GANGSTA RAP PARTY

S'up, homies? You're looking at the only candidate who's a straight up O.G. from the mean streets of Tammerstone. Any punks try and step to us is gon' get got, you feel me?

Ladies and gentlemen, boys and girls. I stand before you a humbled man. After failing to triumph in the film contest, then the food competition, then being part of the football team that so disgracefully lost to Woodlet, I realized that I am in fact . . . not perfect. [GASPS FROM AUDIENCE] I know. I was shocked, too.

But even though I am not perfect, it does not mean that I can't strive to be. And it is in this quest for perfection that I will serve you, the students of Lowes Park.

I am not doing this for fame or for prestige. All I hope is that one day, when pupils are enjoying a top quality education in the Sir Malvern Pope wing of the school, I will be able to come back and visit as prime minister of Great Britain and see what I started on this day. Thank you.

My speech was in my hand, Chuck. I was going to light up the sky telling them all how Awesome I was. But as I listened to Malvern's speech, I realized that wouldn't work. I knew that all the popular kids were going to vote for him anyway and there was no point trying to change their minds. I needed to appeal to the misfits, the losers, the people whose mums write their names on the inside of their pants. If we all mobilize, we could take the election. But first, we had to get past the student council. It is made up of the prefects from every year. They sat at a table at the front of the packed theatre.

Once the massive cheer for Malvern had died down, I stepped up to the lectern.

FREDDIE SMALLHOUSE—THE AWESOMENESS PARTY

I never used to believe that I would amount to anything. Now I see how wrong I was. I have the potential to be whatever I want to be. And so do all of you.

Our school years are our most important. The decisions we make here can have a huge impact on the rest of our lives. And if you elect me as your president, I will make this school a fairer place.

If you get picked last in PE because you're too

fat—I will stand up for you.

If you can't get a date to the dance because of your bad breath, or your love of computer games, or the fact that your nose is constantly bleeding—I will stand up for you.

If you accidentally called a teacher 'Mum' and everyone laughed and threw stuff and said 'but he's a MALE teacher' and then wrote 'Freddie is Mr Norris's baby' on my locker—I will stand up for you.

I want to create a community where everyone is equal and has the same opportunities to get ahead. If that sounds like your idea of a good school, then vote for me, Freddie Smallhouse.

I think I did all right, Chuck. I mean, I kind of got a golf applause afterwards, but I did myself proud. The student council went away for a few minutes to deliberate on the top two.

I was so nervous I couldn't keep my legs still. I glanced over at Malvern, who gave me the stinkeye and mouthed 'I will destroy you' at me.

After about five minutes, the student council

came out of their little room and passed a piece of paper to Mr Bümfacé. It was just like when we watched the jury deliver the verdict to my Grandad for selling smuggled cigarettes to the other residents in his care home.

Mr Bümfacé stood on stage. His hair was all messy and he seemed tired.

'Well,' he said. 'The results of the vote are in, and I am pleased to announce that the two candidates for the Lowes Park Presidential Election are . . .'

He left a dramatic pause, like they do on those reality shows. I got the urge to hold Nilesh's hand but decided against it.

'. . . Malvern Pope of the Malvern Pope Party.'

Most of the room erupted in cheers. Malvern hugged everyone he could get his hands on while I fought the urge to vomit my pancreas.

'And . . .' Mr Bümfacé said when the noise eventually died down.

I sneaked a glance at Charlie Hackensack, who was loosening his tie in anticipation.

'The second candidate is . . .'

I held my breath.

'Freddie Smallhouse of the Awesomeness Party!'

I yelped with joy, expecting a least a small cheer. Nothing.

Literally, the only sound in the entire theatre was me going 'Whoohehehehaaa!'

Everyone was staring. I had never heard a silence like it. Which doesn't even make sense, if you think about it.

'Anyway,' said Bümfacé. 'The election will take place on Friday the seventeenth of April. That gives you one month to convince the voters that your vision for the school is the best one. Good luck.'

Oh my. That's the exact day we're being kicked out of Uncle Barry's. It's going to go right down to the wire.

Malvern swaggered over to me with Lee and Perry in tow.

'I hope you're ready to be beaten,' he said.

'Oh ho ho,' I wiped imaginary tears of laughter from my eyes. 'If anyone is going to be beaten it is you. You right honourable . . . idiot . . . brain.'

We couldn't continue our intelligent debate further because a mob came and swamped Malvern. No one congratulated me. Still, once they hear my policies, they'll come over to my side.

As the crowd began to dissipate, I reached out and shook Nilesh's hand.

'Here's to the next four weeks of campaigning,' I said.

'Can't wait,' he said. 'Really, I can't.'

MESSAGE FROM CHUCK TO ALL HIS AWESOME FOLLOWERS

I would like to take this opportunity to announce my **CHUCK MAKES THE WORLD AN AWESOME PLACE TOUR!** Starting off with the good ol' U.S. of K. Yes, merry Britain, I am coming for you! Dates and prices can be found at my online store, the **AWESOMEPORIUM**.

Yours Awesomely,
Chuck

I can't believe you're actually coming to the UK, Chuck! I feel honoured! I went to the **AWESOMEPORIUM** to look at tickets and unfortunately, there's no way I can afford to go. The cheapest ones for the Birmingham MegaDome show are sixty-five quid. I even asked Uncle Barry if he could lend me the money, but I might as well have been asking for a tap-dancing unicorn. I'm just consoling myself with the knowledge that by the time of your next UK tour, all our problems will be sorted and I will be able to see you.

Our first campaign meeting took place after school in my official campaign centre. Well, I say, campaign centre, it's actually the now-disused school library. When I was walking past Mr Crudwick the caretaker's cupboard, I noticed the keys hanging up so I helped myself. There, I've fulfilled a campaign promise already! Now that's what I call Awesome Efficiency!

My full Campaign Team was there (Me, Nilesh and a couple of spiders). I stood at the head of the table, trying to act all president-like.

'So, team,' I said. 'What intel do we have?'

I've started saying stuff like 'intel' now. I find that shortening words makes you sound proper cle.

'Well, Malvern is already on the offensive,' said Nilesh. He'd spent the day scouring school, for the campaign. 'His posters went up first thing this morning.'

'We have to hit back,' I said. 'Nilesh—you're good at design. I need you to make me a campaign poster.'

Nilesh saluted. 'Do you want me to work some Photoshop magic on your face?'

'No way,' I said. 'I have to show the voters the real me.'

Nilesh grimaced slightly and said. 'Are you sure? Cos I've already done a bit of polling on the subject, and it seems your face is a turn-off for the electorate.'

I gasped. 'My face? What's wrong with my face?'

Nilesh clicked the end of his pen. 'I don't know, but people don't like it. One voter described it as looking like . . . ' He stopped and rifled through some papers. '. . . a dropped flan.'

I didn't know what to say, Chuck. I mean, a dropped flan.

I sighed. 'Fine,' I said. 'Photoshop it is. What else do we have?'

'The Lowes Park Bantz Instagram account has run an informal poll,' said Nilesh. 'It doesn't look good.'

RESULTS

OTHER
1%

MALVERN
99%

@LOWESPARKBANTZ Just as we expected —
Malvern is the best.

'So we have one per cent to work with,' I said.
'It's a start.'

Nilesh laughed. 'There's no way you can turn
that around. It's impossible.'

'Come on, Deputy Leader,' I said. 'Do you
know what Chuck Willard says about the word
impossible?'

'No, but I'm sure you're going to tell me,' he murmured.

'Not just tell you. I'll show you!' I said.

CHUCK'S PEP TALK

Impossible? Nonsense. Add a gap and an apostrophe, and what do you get? I'm possible.

'I'm possible?' said Nilesh. 'That makes literally no sense.'

'Never mind,' I said. 'We have to get started right now if we're going to have any chance. As I mentioned in my speech, we need to target the non-popular kids—I'm talking the emos, the chess club, the metalheads, the boys' choir. We need to find out what they want and promise to give it to them. We have to give a voice to those with no voice, or in the case of the choir, those whose voice is freakishly high and girl-like. And try to get me some coverage on Lowes Park Bantz. It seems like it holds a lot of sway.'

When I got home, I found Dad slumped in

a chair. He'd spent another day job-hunting without getting anywhere. I tried to encourage him to keep going but he said, 'What's the point? I'm a born loser and they can see it. It's in my DNA. In fact, I'd say if you cut me down the middle, you'd see "LOSER" printed through me like a horrible stick of rock.'

I had to try and cheer him up, so I told him about my campaign. Well, he wasn't as enthusiastic as I thought he'd be.

'President?' he said. 'You?'

Honestly, Chuck, he said it like I'd told him I was trying to cross the Sahara Desert on a trike.

'Yes, me,' I said. 'I'm up against Malvern.'

'Of course you are,' said Dad. 'Well, you're wasting your time. Those Popes don't lose. Ever. Besides, when we're kicked out of this place, we'll probably end up in a council flat miles away.'

'So what does that mean?' I said.

Dad dragged his hands down his face and sighed. 'It means you'll probably have to move schools.'

WHAT?! I can't move schools. I mean, I know

Lowes Park isn't exactly the best in the world, but it's what I know. And being the new kid in school is brutal. I remember when Alex Carlton started here a few months ago, some big kids stole his pants from the changing room and covered them in chilli powder.

And I'd never see Nilesh. I'd have no friends. I really need to turn this around, Chuck.

CHUCK'S PEP TALK

At times when things seem darkest, when Awesomeness seems as remote as the tiniest star, remember that you have the ability to win within you. All you have to do is concentrate really hard and you will find it. Go ahead, do it now. Focus really hard on your insides until you see it. Found it yet? No, that's your small intestine, just to the left of that. There it is. Now let it grow within you. Now it's bigger than your pancreas, now your heart, now your liver. Now it's so big, Awesomeness is bursting out of your ears! Now get out there and let the world see the Awesomeness that is leaking out of your every orifice!

Well Chuck, I decided that the best approach is to go full steam ahead with my campaign. I'm not going to beat Malvern by sitting around moping. I have to take action.

At lunchtime, I went down to the basement and chatted with the various subcultures that exist here at Lowes Park:

I noted down all their concerns and comments (mainly 'leave me alone, you freak') and added them to my file. I felt like I had secured at least a few votes. At lunch, I arranged to speak to the chess club, in their corner of the basement. Thing is, Chuck, I've never played chess in my life, so I had to have a quick google first.

'Ladies and . . . ah, sorry, gentlemen. Just gentlemen of the Lowes Park chess club, I come to you today to give you a glimpse of a better future. A future where you don't have to be pawns. You can be kings or que—sorry, just kings. No longer will you just be able to move one square at a time. You will stride across the chess board of life in all directions, taking people's knights and stealing their castles.'

I stopped and looked at their faces. One of them had his hand over his mouth because he was so stunned. Or he was yawning, one or the other.

'I guess what I'm trying to say is, if you vote for me, I will be your voice, and your pasty skin, bad posture, and lack of social skills will no longer hold you back.' I pointed at a kid in the front row. 'You there. Tell me your name and your biggest ambition.'

'Um,' he said. 'My name is Toby Marston and I would like to be an engineer.'

'You can!' I said. 'Next!'

'My name is Gareth Stockford and I want to write children's books.'

'Kind of a lame job, but if it's what you want, great,' I said. 'Next.'

'My name is Colin Roctor and I want to be a brain surgeon.'

'Grea—' I stopped myself mid-word when I realized what he'd said. 'Wait a minute, isn't a brain surgeon a kind of doctor?'

'Well, yes,' he said.

I giggled to myself. 'So your name would be Doctor Roctor?'

'Yes,' said Colin. 'What's so funny about that?'

'Are you serious?' I said. '"Doctor Roctor is ready to operate on your brain now." No thanks, I'd rather take my chances with a

Black and Decker and some chloroform. That is HILARIOUS.'

I laughed, expecting everyone else to join in. They didn't. Quite the opposite.

Ugh, I'm really going to need to bring in some strong pro-chess policies if I have any hope of winning them back.

CHUCK'S PEP TALK

Remember: When things are going wrong, it's important to keep your chin up. My chin is permanently at a 120 degree angle and I feel great!

We had another meeting at Campaign HQ after school. I started by asking Nilesh if he'd managed to get anything about me on Bantz.

'I didn't have to,' he replied. 'You're already on it.'

@LOWESPARKBANTZ Smallhouse too busy playing golf with weird dad to concentrate on campaign.

I punched my palm. 'Malvern,' I growled. 'He's behind this whole thing.'

'I suspected as much,' said Nilesh. 'Look at this.'

@LOWESPARKBANTZ Malvern Pope has a perfect academic record

'He's probably got all kinds of connections, so I'd say it's only a matter of time before he tracks yours down,' Nilesh went on. 'How are your grades, anyway?'

I gulped. 'Good. But not perfect.'

'How so?' said Nilesh.

'I got a U in Drama last year.'

Nilesh gawped at me. 'I thought it was basically impossible to fail Drama.'

I shook my head. 'I messed up my line in Hamlet, remember? I just really needed a wee.'

@LOWESPARKBANTZ Shakespeare definitely didn't write, 'to pee or not to pee.'

'Be that as it may,' said Nilesh, 'you should be prepared for Bantz or Malvern or whoever to use this against you.'

I sat down in my presidential chair and pondered. 'There has to be a way of changing them,' I said.

'Doubt it,' said Nilesh. 'Plus, that seems kind of unethical.'

I shushed him as I pulled out the laptop and went to the Lowes Park top secret invite-only student Facebook page. The fact that I only got in there in the first place because I was posing as a handsome American exchange student is by-the-by. Anyway, after a quick search I (Chad McStarsnstripes) managed to find a thread about the Fixer. Apparently, he's this mystery kid who can hack into the school's computer system and change your grades.

They say he hangs around in the basement before school. But you have to be cool. Too obvious and he walks away. Some people were saying that he doesn't exist and is just a school myth, but I have to at least try.

'Don't even think about it,' said Nilesh, peeking over my shoulder.

'Why not?' I said. 'Malvern already has an unfair advantage over me with this Bantz thing. I'm just levelling the playing field.'

Nilesh sighed. 'Look, I've gone along with a lot of your weird ideas lately, but I can't do this.'

I growled under my breath. I didn't get why he was being like that. He knows full well what's at stake.

'Fine,' I said. 'You don't have to do anything. Just leave it to me.'

Look, Chuck, I know it's not cool to cheat, but when the odds are stacked against you, you have to bend the rules a little.

CHUCK'S PEP TALK

If you ever find yourself in the grip of a moral dilemma, you only have to ask yourself one question: What would Chuck do?

Later on, I went into the lounge. I still wasn't a hundred per cent sure about the whole Fixer thing. Nilesh had thrown a spanner in the works with his lousy 'ethics'.

Mum, Dad, and Uncle Barry were sitting in the lounge, watching the lottery results on TV. Well, Mum and Uncle Barry were. Dad was lying face down on the carpet.

Mum had a big stack of lottery tickets she was frantically checking through. Uncle Barry had one. Mum ripped all of hers up, one-by-one.

'What did I tell you, Sandra?' said Dad, his voice muffled by the floor. 'There will be no miracle for us.'

Mum sighed. 'I spent my entire bonus on those tickets.'

Uncle Barry chuckled to himself and kissed his solitary ticket. 'Victory for Barry,' he said. 'Ten English pounds which I can convert to Euros.'

'Congratulations,' Mum said, half-heartedly.

'Yeah, we're all really happy for you, Barry,' said Dad.

That decided it. If Mum is getting so desperate that she's resorting to buying loads of lottery tickets, I have to win this election. Forget ethics, I need the Fixer.

MESSAGE FROM CHUCK

Hey British fans,

Just to let you know that the UK leg of my

CHUCK MAKES THE WORLD AN

AWESOME PLACE tour is SOLD OUT. Boy, you

Brits really love the Chuck. And you should, because I'm going

to show you that you can be **AWESOME**, despite your

flabby physiques and terrible teeth.

Tatty bye, my crumpets!

Chuck

THE FIXER

I didn't get much sleep last night. I was too busy tossing and turning, worrying about what was going to happen when I found the Fixer, and stressing out about any other skeletons in my closet that Lowes Park Bantz/Malvern might find. What if they discover that me and Nilesh are the ones behind Mr and Mrs Barrington's crazy channel-changing TV? And we'd used that long-range universal Switchyswitch remote at school, too. Who could forget that History lesson last year?

I got to school early and headed straight to the basement. It was pretty full with all the nerdy clubs in school. It's dingy and a little scary, but it's the only place these kids can indulge their interests without getting wedgies.

I had no idea what this Fixer looked like, so I was going to have to use my best judgement. I checked in all the little side rooms, but all the kids in there looked too nervous to be the Fixer. But when I got to the back of the room, I saw him. I just knew it was him. He coolly leaned against the wall while other kids sat on the floor, hunched over boards. He looked dark and mysterious, his eyes half closed and a little smile on his lips.

I sidled over and stood next to him, mimicking his lean. I decided to get straight to the point.

I said, 'How much for an A?'

He said, 'One point.'

I said, 'What are you talking about?'

He said, 'This is Scrabble club.'

I said, 'Oh.'

He said, 'Yeah, that's one point as well.'

I said, 'I see.'

He said, 'Get out.'

I said, 'Why?'

So it seems the Fixer isn't real. And that's not the worst of my troubles.

♡

@LOWESPARKBANTZ Corrupt Smallhouse attempts to buy grade from scrabble club!

Damn, how did he know? I called an emergency meeting at HQ to try and control the damage.

'Come on, Deputy Leader,' I said, clicking my fingers. 'I need ideas, fast.'

Nilesh sighed. 'If you'd listened to me, you wouldn't have gone looking for the "Fixer" in the first place.'

'Now is not the time for "I told you sos" or air quotes,' I said. 'Come on, there must be something we can do.'

Nilesh rolled his eyes and sat back in his chair. 'The way I see it, we need a distraction. You see it time and time again at school. Remember when Danny Tromans spilled a can of coke in his lap and it looked like he weed himself and the only way he could stop everyone laughing was to say, "Hey, remember when Nilesh actually weed himself?" You need something like that.'

I narrowed my eyes. 'So you're saying I need to accuse Malvern of peeing his pants?'

'No,' Nilesh groaned. 'Just do something to make people forget about the Fixer scandal.

Maybe something to show everyone that you're a good person. Something that will improve the school.'

I paced around HQ and thought about it. What would improve the school? Everyone I asked talked about how bad the sports facilities are. I mean, I heard that the hockey team is having to use stale baguettes for sticks, and I know for a fact that our swimming pool is empty. Plus, just last month, a visiting rugby team from Atherworth Academy contracted a rare tropical illness from the boys' changing rooms.

There are loads of kids that play sports and if I promise to improve the facilities, that could win plenty of votes. Just because I can't play sports doesn't mean I can't help those who can.

Nilesh and I put our heads together and planned a Sports Manifesto. The idea was we'd take photos of the existing facilities and combine them with Photoshopped artist's impressions of how they'd look with our improvements.

I "borrowed" Uncle Barry's new fancy camera and stashed it in my wardrobe. It would make the shots hi-res and super professional. Tomorrow, we'll take them. We have to act fast if we want to save my campaign.

CHUCK'S PEP TALK

Taking photos is for suckers. Why not just sign up for access to the Chuck Willard Stock Photo Archive?

For the low, low price of $299.99, you will get unlimited access to all my stock photos. You'll find something there for every occasion! Here's one of a workin' man!

I got into school this morning to find my
campaign posters up on every corridor.

'Nice job,' I said to Nilesh. 'And you didn't have to resort to Photoshopping after all.'

Nilesh looked like he was going to lie but then thought better of it. 'Actually I did.'

'Really?' I said, leaning forward to inspect it closer. 'What did you do?'

He said, 'Maybe I made your eyes a bit less . . . close together.'

I was about to argue that my eyes are definitely not too close together, but then I remembered my last trip to the opticians.

Still, at least I look photogenic for once. HA! Take that Year Six class photographer! Make me stand behind a potted plant, will you?

At lunchtime, I headed down to the PE department to photograph the changing rooms. I had checked the rota and saw no clubs using the field so I knew they would be free. To be safe, though, I got Nilesh to stand guard outside to warn me if any teachers showed up.

I took Uncle Barry's expensive camera straight into the boys' room and quickly got to work, photographing the cracks in the walls, the rusty clothes pegs and the rat traps.

'This should give me plenty to work with,' I said to myself.

But not enough.

See, Chuck, I wanted to appeal to ALL sporty kids, including girls. And how could I do that if I only concentrated on the male facilities?

But still, could I really enter the mystery world of the girls' changing room? Nobody knows what is behind that door. Well, girls do, but you know what I mean.

To help make my mind up, I pulled my tablet out of the bag and consulted the Awesomeness app to see if you had any words of wisdom for me. Of course you did!

CHUCK'S PEP TALK

If you're wondering whether to take a leap into the unknown—always do it!

LEGAL NOTICE: This is referring to metaphorical leaps only. Chuck accepts no responsibility for any cliff- or bridge-based tragedies.

That settled it. I quickly ducked out of the boys' room and into the corridor. I was about to enter the girls' room when I felt a hand on my shoulder.

'What the hell are you doing?' Nilesh hissed.

I turned around. 'I have to be president for ALL students.'

His eyes went huge. 'But that's the girls' changing room.'

'And?' I said. 'Are we not all the same, beneath our uniforms?'

'No!' Nilesh cried. 'Very much no!'

'Oh yeah,' I said. 'Look, it's fine, it'll be empty.'

'Don't do this, Freddie,' Nilesh warned.

I gave him a 'step aside' look and went inside.

Immediately, I was struck by the difference. It was spotless. There were no cracks in the walls, no missing hooks, and it didn't smell like the meeting of a B.O. support group.

'I wish I was a girl,' I whispered to myself.

In a weird way, though I was kind of annoyed by their cleanliness. Surely there had to be some imperfections, otherwise what was I going to photograph?

I stepped into the toilet cubicle. Bingo. Someone had dropped a sheet of toilet paper on the floor. I did a quick check, but no, it was clean.

A noise from outside made my heart race. I quickly slammed the door shut and locked it.

I listened for further noises. There were voices. Definite voices.

Girls' voices.

There was no way out. I had to wait in the cubicle until they left. I held my breath and tried to stay perfectly still. I didn't understand, the rota said the field wasn't in use. Then I remembered: the sports hall! I didn't think to check the sports hall rota! I thought it was still closed. They must have cleared the black mould and reopened it.

Despite the terror surging through my veins, I was slightly curious to hear what girls get up to in the changing rooms.

'God, I am sweating like a beast.'

'I know, I can smell you from here.'

Well that was disappointing. If it wasn't for their sweet voices you'd think it was a gang of hairy bricklayers.

I carefully sat down on the toilet and tucked my legs up. I didn't want anyone to see my less than girly size eights under the door. I could stay put until they went. No one would ever need know I was there.

'It's no good, girls, I need a dump!'

WHAT? All I could hear was everyone groaning and my own brain screaming. There was only one cubicle in the changing room.

The door rattled.

NO NO NOOOOO!

'There someone in there?'

I stayed perfectly still.

The door rattled again. 'Come on, who is it?'

I didn't even want to blink, in case my eyelids were too loud.

'OK, this is freaking me out now, because everyone is out here.'

'Oh my God, Lorna, get away. It could be an axe murderer in there.'

'We should call Ms Stirch.'

I cleared my throat. 'No, it's OK,' I said in a terrible old lady voice. 'It's just me, the cleaner.'

A low murmur rippled around the room.

'Why have you locked the door if you're cleaning?'

Damn. Stupid girls and their stupid logic. 'I'm, uh, not cleaning, dear. I'm using the, um, facilities. Ooh, mushy peas go right through me.'

There was a pause that seemed to stretch on for hours.

'That ain't the cleaner.'

Plop! Ploppy plop plop!
Superploppafragalisticexpiplopidocious!

'Yeah, my Auntie Beryl is the cleaner and she doesn't talk like that.'

'Yes I do,' I said. 'You're my favourite niece.'

'What's my name, then?'

I let out a silent scream. This was the worst thing to ever happen to anyone.

'Rosie?'

Someone banged on the door.

'Get out of there, right now.'

'I can't, I really am pooing! Listen . . . pllllllllllllllllll.'

It went quiet. Until someone said, 'That's it, let me get on your shoulders.'

I screwed my eyes shut. I thought maybe if I wished hard enough, I could just pop out of existence.

Didn't work.

I looked up and saw Janelle Andrews glaring down at me with hellacious fury in her eyes.

'It's that freak that's standing in the election!' she screamed. 'And he's got a camera!'

'No! I can explain!' I cried. 'This is for my campaign!'

'PERVERT!'

'GET HIM!'

DISGRACE

Everything is unAwesome, Chuck. Everything!

I am now a disgraced politician. I mean, yes, Mr Bümfacé did accept my explanation but the damage is done. My reputation is in tatters, and only Mr Crudwick and his mop could save me from being torn apart by the sixth form girls' netball team.

To make matters worse, Uncle Barry's camera got smashed in the melée and having to tell him about it was not a pleasant job.

'I am most displeased about this, Frederick. I let you into my home and you repay me by taking my property without permission and destroying it? Do you have any idea how many photographs of parking violations I had on there? Lost forever. Think of all the law-breaking motorists that are going to get away with their indiscretions.'

I gulped and stared at the floor. It was like being told off by a disgruntled owl with halitosis.

'Um, sorry?'

'Well, sorry just isn't going to cut it, young man,' said Uncle Barry. 'You owe me a camera of equal or superior specification before I leave for Germany.'

There's no way I'm going to be able to afford a fancy new camera. And what's he going to do? Not go to Germany until I pay it off?

'I daresay if you had more parental discipline, things like this wouldn't happen.' He nodded at Dad who was picking bits of old food out of his beard. Mum wasn't even in because she was pulling a double shift at work.

Dad looked up from his beard pickings. 'Ah give over, Barry,' he said. 'Did you never get up to mischief when you were a boy?'

'Never,' said Uncle Barry.

From what Mum told me, it sounds like the truth. Apparently, when they were both still in primary school, she picked some flowers from the riverside and he reported her to the Environment Agency.

This is no good, Chuck. I have to figure out a

way to rescue my campaign. I decided to go for a walk to help me think. Without intending to, I ended up back on my old road, walking past Nilesh's, the Barringtons', and Malvern's house (named 'the Vatican'). I took a quick peep into our old house. A new family have moved in and they were sitting at the table having dinner. They were smiling, chatting and laughing. Then looking out of the window wondering who the weird kid behind the bush was.

Eventually, I wound my way back to the street I live on now. It's depressing, having to go back. And the thing is, Chuck, it's not even because the house isn't as nice—I could live with that. It's the fact that it's Uncle Barry's, and he's kicking us out.

I was about to head back in when I heard a 'Hey, kid.' I turned around and saw Heavy Metal Steve with his dog, Keith.

'Hi Heavy Metal Steve,' I said, half-heartedly. 'How's the rocking business?'

'Wicked, man,' he said. 'The other night Furious Gibbon played Wembley.'

'Wow,' I said. 'Arena or stadium?'

'No, not Wembley,' he said. 'Weobley. Biggest village in Herefordshire. We rocked the Miners' Welfare like there was no tomorrow.'

Those poor Weobleyans.

'I noticed your Uncle Barry's finally sold up,' he said, nodding at the sign. 'Hopefully the new neighbours will be more in tune with my rock 'n' roll vibe. So are you going with him, or what?'

'No,' I said. 'We're probably going to end up in a B&B.'

Heavy Metal Steve winced. 'Ouch,' he said. 'That's rough, little dude. Say, do you want to earn some extra cash?'

'Yes,' I said. 'Definitely.' Then I recoiled a bit because I had no idea what he wanted me to do. His car looked like it hadn't been washed since before I was born so I wasn't keen on the idea of tackling that.

'Why don't you walk Keith for me?' he said. 'You're mates with Mittens so you've got solid experience. I'll pay you a fiver a day.'

OK, so it's not the kind of Awesome job that would solve all our problems, but it's a start. 'I'll take it,' I said.

He smiled and handed me the lead. 'Great. You can start now. Go on, Keith.'

We walked for a while and I relaxed when I realized that this dog was way calmer than Mittens. Even though he really looked like him. Same breed, same colouring. The only difference is, Keith has one ear a little bit bigger than the other and his eyes face different directions. Like, totally different directions.

We walked along the canal and ended up in the park. I decided to let him off the lead for a bit so we could play Fetch. I picked up a stick and threw it. 'Go on, Keith, fetch it!'

He took off across the park the wrong way and came back with an empty beer can.

'You're a strange one, aren't you boy?' I said. He looked back at me (well, I think he did. Like I say, his eyes are all over the place) and dropped the can as if he expected me to throw it. I did, but then he ran off and came back with the stick I threw in the first place. I was beginning to see why Heavy Metal Steve didn't fancy walking him.

'Hey, Smallhouse!'

I screwed my eyes shut. I could recognize that voice anywhere.

'What do you want, Malvern?'

Malvern and his two goon friends, Lee Fields and Perry Crofts were stood under a tree. Malvern held up one of my campaign posters.

'Nothing,' he said. 'Just stocking up on toilet paper.'

'Hey,' I said. 'That's for my campaign, you're not supposed to touch that!'

'What are you going to do about it, Smalhouse?' he said. 'Sneak into my bathroom and take photos of me?'

'Give it back!' I yelled.

Malvern and the others just laughed at me.

'That's it,' I said, pointing right at them. 'Get them, boy!'

Keith took off across the park, and jumped on Malvern, knocking him to the floor and making him screech like a wimpy parrot. Wow, he can actually do as he's asked. He even grabbed the poster off Malvern and started bringing it back.

Then he stopped, dropped it on the floor and started digging at it with his front paws until it was torn into a hundred pieces. Then he peed on it.

Well, he kind of looks like Mittens and he can kind of follow orders. Maybe he can be of some use to my campaign. Wait a second. Maybe he can be REALLY useful to my campaign.

CHUCK'S PEP TALK

Chuck's Recipe for Success
1 tablespoon of Determination.
A cup of Style.
A dash of Entrepreneurship.
And one truckload of **AWESOMENESS**.

'No way,' said Nilesh at the school gate this morning. 'I will have no part of this.'

'Why not?' I said. 'Look, he's exactly like him!' Heavy Metal Steve gave me a spare key so I can fetch Keith after he'd leaves for work, so I decided to borrow him for the day.

'Because it's completely dishonest,' said Nilesh. 'Plus, look at him—his eyes are all wonky.'

I clamped my hands over Keith's ears. 'Will you be quiet?' I said. 'He's very sensitive about his eyeballs.'

Prawn McKenzie, who happened to be walking past, stopped and pointed at Keith. 'Hold on a minute, is that Mittens?'

I gave Nilesh a look, then confirmed that it was indeed the hero dog.

'Cool,' Prawn gasped. 'Can I have a selfie with him?'

Nilesh gawped at us as if he couldn't believe

what he was seeing. Afterwards, he said to me, 'Yeah, but that was Prawn McKenzie. He thought that bloke that burgled his house was really Santa Claus.'

As soon as he'd said it, Kacie Kelly and Amaia Bletchley turned up, going, 'Oh my God, I can't believe Mittens is here!'

So basically, I was the talk of the school today, Chuck. Everybody wanted a piece of the Mittens action. Nilesh didn't approve, but the way I saw it, I was doing a good thing. People were excited and proud to be Lowes Parkians. The only time we'd had a brush with fame before was when *Crimewatch* filmed some reconstructions here. Mr Bümfacé was so starstruck, he didn't even complain about a dog being in his school. I mean, he actually curtsied when he saw him.

Malvern came and found me at lunch and got in my face. 'I don't know how you did this,' he said. 'But I am going to get you back for it. Mark my words.'

I didn't care, Chuck, because I knew he was only saying it because he was scared. Latest opinion polls put me at 25% approval, which is a huge increase. A few more days of 'Mittens' and I'll be in the lead. Dad's new job is within reach, I just know it.

Have you joined my program, watched my TV shows, and read my books and still don't feel **AWESOME**?

Sounds like you need

CHUCK'S AWESOME PILLS!

Take two a day and you will feel perky, fresh and ready for anything.
And the only side effect is
AWESOMENESS!

WARNING: real side effects may include shortness of breath, incontinence, halitosis, acne, delusions of grandeur, spontaneous human combustion, the bubonic plague, blindness, death, and sore throat.

What a day, Chuck. I was feeling tired but satisfied after my day with Keith. I'd received my wages and invested them wisely (in my official Chuck Willard Piggy Bank). I told Dad about my job, expecting him to be pleased, but he just said, 'GREAT. MY THIRTEEN-YEAR-OLD SON CAN GET GAINFUL EMPLOYMENT, BUT I CAN'T!'

Just wait until I win this election. Then I'll show him. He'll be my old Dad again. And I'm sure all the kids will love him. He's clever, he's funny, he's good at sports. He'll be the best teacher of all time.

Anyway, picture the scene, Chuck. It's lunchtime today. Nilesh and I had to leave the dining hall and eat our sandwiches outside because Keith could see us from where he was chained up and kept running head first into the window.

Nilesh was still a bit peeved about me

pretending Keith was Mittens, but I ignored it. I mean, Nilesh is my best friend, but just lately he's got too hung up on 'ethics' and 'morals'. I guess it's easy to have stuff like that when you have a nice house and aren't about to be homeless. Plus, he needs to stop going on about the Epic Warfare tournament all the time. Can't he see I have more important things to worry about?

I was just trying to stop Keith from eating my lunch when a stampede pushed past us. Me and Nilesh exchanged a look and followed, leaving Keith chained up. The crowd was streaming towards the outside entrance to the theatre. When we got there, there was already a heaving throng, chanting, 'Let us in, let us in.'

I tried to ask people what they were waiting for, but it was as if I wasn't there. They were all focussed on the door. When it finally opened, there was nearly a crush. Through the scrum, I saw Lee and Perry drag a bin out, then help Malvern onto it.

'Silence!' he yelled. Everyone did as they were told instantly.

'There is limited space in this theatre, so I will personally select who is allowed in. Now one at a time, step up to Lee and Perry, and so help me God, if you argue, I will have you escorted off the premises,' Malvern said.

I still didn't know what any of this was for, but everyone seemed dead keen to get in. I knew there was no way Malvern was going to let me in, so I wriggled out of the crush and got a better view from the outside.

Malvern was inspecting people one-by-one.

'OK, you're in.'

'You're out.'

'Wait a second, didn't you once pee yourself in class? OUT!'

Some of the rejected people trudged my way, looking like they might actually cry.

'What's the matter?' I asked. 'What's happening in there?'

Bridget Meyers, captain of the mathletics club looked at me and said, 'He's got Midlake Darston in there.'

I gulped. Surely not THE Midlake Darston? One

of the most famous YouTubers in the world? A boy so handsome, he makes girls faint when they look at him? Surely not him?

Nilesh pulled his phone out and nodded. 'It wouldn't surprise me,' he said. 'According to his Twitter feed, he's doing a corporate gig for MorganKemptonSchneffleberger this afternoon. I bet Malvern Sr paid him extra to come here and give Junior's campaign a boost.'

After the chosen ones had filed in, I jostled for position by the window and watched as the one and only Midlake Darston appeared on stage. I couldn't believe it, Chuck. He saw that I had a national celebrity on my team and had to go one better and get an INTERnational celebrity. People around me started banging the glass and screaming Midlake's name, but then Perry drew the curtains and Lee chased them off.

I felt bad for them, Chuck. It was as if Malvern was telling them they weren't good enough. After losing our house, it's how I've felt. And it's definitely how Dad has felt. I ran and clambered on top of the bin.

'Everybody!' I shouted. 'I'm very sorry you missed out on seeing Midlake. As an alternative, I've arranged a Meet-and-Greet with Mittens in the library, come one, come all.'

There were a few shrugs and 's'pose so's, but people came up. And you know what, Chuck? It was great. The chess club was there, the mathletes were out in force, even the goths and the emos put aside their differences to pay their respects to the great dog. Keith was on good form, too, and appreciated the fuss, when he wasn't eating the complete works of Charles Dickens. It was as if he'd made them forget that I was a perv who sneaks into girls' changing rooms.

At the end of lunch, I couldn't see anyone looking sad any more. Colin Roctor even stopped me on the way out and said, 'This was great. When's the next Losers' Club?'

And as soon as he said it, a new idea was born.

CHUCK'S PEP TALK

If you're not lucky enough to live in SoCal like I am, you're going to need some help with your skin game. So why not try Chuck's Awesome Fake Tan? Ranging from 'Light Ochre' to 'Dark Chocolate', I've got a shade for every occasion!*

*Chuck accepts no responsibility for any permanent staining of furniture, wallpaper or loved ones.

★ 185 ★

'So I guess this isn't Campaign HQ any more,' said Nilesh as I pinned the sign to the library door.

LOSERS' CLUB

Here every lunchtime.

Open to EVERYONE.

'It makes sense to have it in here,' I said. 'These people have had to hide down in the basement for months. I'm going to create a space for them to be themselves above ground.'

'What's the end game of all this, anyway?' said Nilesh.

'To win,' I said. 'I don't REALLY care about chess and board games or whatever they're all into, but I do care about the people. If I can hear their concerns, I can win them over and it will only mean good things for the campaign.'

Nilesh still didn't look convinced.

'Listen,' I said. 'If we mobilize all the types of people Malvern wouldn't let into his precious celebrity party, we can take it. Imagine this school with the losers running the show. It'll turn it on its head! I'll achieve exactly what I set out in my speech.'

As planned, everyone from the day before showed up. They brought all their stuff, too—chessboards, D&D packs, Pokémon cards. And treats. So many treats. They all had something for Mittens/Keith. It really was the nerdy safe space I had imagined.

Nilesh brought the PC version of Epic Warfare

in and loaded it up on one of the computers, too. He tried to get me to play, but I was mostly too busy networking with all my new friends/voters.

Over the past couple of days, it has got bigger and bigger. Some of the Live Action Role Players even brought their costumes in. The whole school seemed to be a more cheerful place. And it wasn't just me saying that. Mr Bümfacé came and found me and said teachers had noticed vast improvements in the classroom. If the Mittens effect continued, grades would definitely go up. He said he wanted to hold a special assembly to honour Mittens and invite the local press. It would be great publicity for the school. Much better than we usually get.

Tammerstone Times ONLINE

🏠 | NEWS | SPORT | WHAT'S ON | ANNOUNCEMENTS | BUY & SELL | 🔍

LOWES PARK: LAST IN MATHS, FIRST IN CRIME

Today, though, was a bit different. I was halfway through trying to convince some emos that life isn't all that bad after all, when everyone went silent. I turned around, and there was Malvern, flanked by Lee and Perry.

'And just what is going on here?' Malvern seethed.

I turned around and gave him my best presidential smile. 'Sorry, Malvern,' I said. 'You're not allowed in here. I'm going to have to ask you to leave.'

Malvern's face went purple. 'How very dare you!' he yelped. 'You can't ban me from anywhere!'

'I'm afraid I can,' I said. 'You stopped these wonderful people from entering the theatre to see Midlake Darston, so I'm stopping you from coming in here.'

'Fine,' Malvern shouted. 'If I can't come in, all of you should leave.' He gestured around the room. 'Come on, move it.'

No one stirred.

'Lee, Perry,' he said, 'get all these freaks out of here.'

Lee and Perry looked at each other, but didn't move. 'I don't know, Malvern,' said Perry. 'They've got Pokémon.'

'Yeah,' said Lee. 'Pokémon's wicked.'

Malvern gasped. 'Are you disobeying my orders?'

They didn't speak. The room was dead silent.

Malvern started shoving them, but it was like a gerbil trying to move a lorry.

'You do not disobey me, you pair of stinking apes,' Malvern squeaked. 'I am Malvern Pope— your social superior.'

Lee and Perry gave each other a look, then Lee picked him up, Perry got the door and they dumped him out on the corridor. The whole way, he was yelling stuff like, 'I can win this election without you freaks, anyway.' Then Perry propped a chair under the door handle and they went to join a Pokémon game.

Malvern hammered on the door, screaming, 'I'M GOING TO GET YOU FOR THIS, SMALLHOUSE!'

I'd like to see him try, Chuck. The latest polls

have us neck-and-neck. I'm going to overtake him any day now, I just know it.

CHUCK'S PEP TALK

From the second I was born, I was already half Awesome.
I was screaming, 'AWWWWEEE', which is only one syllable away.
Needless to say, I was king of pre-school.

The Losers' Club is getting better by the day,
Chuck. The choir wrote a song called 'Mittens's
Aria.' And you should have seen what the crochet
club made.

Of course, Lowes Park Bantz were trying to
derail it by taking photos of the LARPers and
using them out of context.

♡

@LOWESPARKBANTZ So-called 'Losers club' is a training camp for Vikings.

And yes, we've had our share of opposition from the 'cool kids', but my new security detail of Lee and Perry sorts that out.

Due to popular demand, I've even started an after-school Losers' Club. Home is miserable and Heavy Metal Steve doesn't get home 'til six, so it's fine by me.

But it's not fine by everyone. At about half three today, Nilesh stormed in.

'What are you doing here?' he said. 'We're supposed to be practising for the Epic Warfare tournament this weekend.'

I screwed my eyes shut. I had completely forgotten about that.

'But I can see you have more important things

to worry about,' he said, looking around the room at the packed out Losers' Club.

'I'm sorry Nilesh,' I said. 'I'm just giving the people what they want. I read about it in Chuck Willard's book, *Supply the Awesome, Demand the Awesome*.'

'I don't want to hear about Chuck Willard ever again,' said Nilesh. 'The man is an idiot.'

'Hey, wait a minute,' I said, but he cut me off and gestured at Lee and Perry, standing either side of me with their arms folded.

'I mean, what's this all about?' he said. 'Are they wearing hearing aids? Where did you get those?'

'Never mind,' I said. 'And they're earpieces, like what the president's secret service wear.'

'You're not president, though,' said Nilesh.

'Not yet,' I fired back. 'But with support like this, there's no way I can lose.'

I just wish he'd stop being such a wet blanket, Chuck. I'm on the cusp of something genuinely Awesome and he does nothing but whinge. I'm sure he'll come around when he's vice president. And if he doesn't, well, I can always find someone else.

CHUCK'S PEP TALK

When you're top dog, you can't be afraid to make tough decisions. I fired three people this morning before breakfast. INCLUDING my chef. And I don't feel guilty about it. In fact, other than my scrambled eggs having an odd consistency, everything is **AWESOME**!

THE ASSEMBLY

One week until the election, Chuck. And that means one week until we get kicked out of Uncle Barry's house. Latest numbers have me with a five per cent lead. All I have to do is maintain it and not screw up.

Today was the special assembly to celebrate Mittens's positive impact on Lowes Park.

Mr Bümfacé had gone all out. There were banners, flags, bunting. A big sign that said, 'Thank You Mittans.' (It wasn't spell-checked).

Everyone was in the theatre. Literally everyone in school. Plus, there was a photographer from the local paper. I stood backstage with Mittens/Keith. I asked Nilesh to come up with me, but he refused, saying something about how it was dishonest and blah, blah, blah, so it looked like it was just me.

Mr Bümfacé came by to make sure we were ready. He dabbed his sweaty forehead and left thin strips of tissue hanging there like horrible streamers. He didn't even notice when he stepped up to the lectern to speak and had no idea why people were laughing.

'Boys and girls,' he began. 'It is an honour and a privilege to welcome you here to this very special assembly in honour of a very special dog. Please give a big round of applause to Mittens.'

The crowd went crazy. Well, half of them did. Malvern's cool crew stayed silent. I stepped up to the lectern, my heart pounding, and tried to remember everything you said about public speaking.

CHUCK'S PEP TALK

If you're ever nervous in front of someone, remember they put their pants on one leg at a time, just like you. Not like me, though. I have people to do that for me.

'Hello everyone,' I said. 'It has been brilliant bringing the very famous Mittens to Lowes Park. So many of you have said how you felt honoured to be in his presence, and so do I.'

I looked out and saw Nilesh staring at the floor with his arms folded.

'Not only is Mittens a hero for saving that old army bloke, he's also a hero for how good he has made us all feel.'

'STOP RIGHT THERE!'

Oh no.

I turned around and there was Malvern, mic in hand, fury in his eyes. He pushed past me on his way to the front of the stage.

'This is not Mittens at all,' he yelled. 'This dog is an IMPOSTER!'

A murmur rippled around the room. Mr Bümfacé looked like he was going to faint. Then he did faint. I looked down at Keith, who was happily chewing on his own bum as if he didn't have a care in the world.

Malvern pressed a button on a little remote and the screen lowered from the ceiling.

'Exhibit A,' he said. 'The photo on the left is Mittens. The photo on the right is Keith.'

'Clearly a different dog!' Malvern yelled.

I didn't know what to do, Chuck. When he said he'd get me, I didn't think he actually would. I glanced at Nilesh, whose face was somehow a mixture of horror and 'I told you so'.

'Exhibit B,' Malvern went on, striding across the stage. 'Mittens's Twitter feed.'

@TheGENUINEMittens Great to be in LA meeting producers of Mittens the Movie! #blessed

'How indeed,' said Malvern. 'Can this dog be in two places, nay, two countries at once?'

I gulped and stayed quiet.

'Exhibit C.'

'By following Smallhouse after school and tracking his movements, I discovered that this dog belongs to a gentleman by the name of Stephen Bagshaw, or "Heavy Metal Steve". And he is not called Mittens at all. His name . . . is Keith!' he boomed.

It went silent. Everyone stared at me. Malvern jabbed my arm and said, 'Go on, Smallhouse. Explain yourself.'

The problem was, I couldn't, Chuck. He had

me bang to rights. I had lied to everyone. This was it—the end. My campaign was finished. Dead. I would lose the election, Dad wouldn't get his job at the school, and we would be living in a grotty B&B for the rest of our lives.

'Leave it out, Malvern,' said Lulu McGregor, leader of the crochet club.

'Yeah, shut up,' said Colin Roctor.

Malvern looked like he'd stepped into a parallel dimension.

'What are you talking about?' he yelped frantically. 'Smallhouse is dishonest—he tricked you!'

'No he didn't,' said Raven Lucretia, head goth. 'We all knew that wasn't really Mittens.'

What?

'Are you KIDDING ME?' Malvern screamed.

'How stupid do you think we are?' said Naeema Kumar, *Carcassonne* captain. 'Only an idiot would believe that dog was Mittens.'

'Yeah,' said Ashley Hitchens, champion knitter. 'I mean, Mittens wouldn't spend an entire afternoon trying to eat his own ear.'

Malvern's face went purple, then white, then a pale shade of green. 'I don't understand,' he whispered. 'Why don't you care that he was tricking you?'

'If I may,' said Bridget Meyers, the mathlete, standing up. 'When you refused to allow us into the Midlake Darston event, you made us feel like a bunch of losers. This false Mittens gave us somewhere to go, somewhere to feel accepted. He showed us that even though you might have wonky ears and weird eyes and know pi to a thousand decimal places but can get lost in your own street, you can still be loved and appreciated.'

I was a little bit choked, to be honest, Chuck. I had no idea we were having that kind of effect on people.

'So in the election next week, I will be placing my vote for Freddie Smallhouse,' she said.

The crowd (well, half of them anyway) roared and applauded. Malvern screamed and ran at me, attacking me with a series of weak slaps that was like being assaulted by an elderly moth. Before he

could work up a real head of steam, Lee and Perry
stepped in and ejected him from the theatre,
to even more cheers and a 'Keith' chant. Keith
responded by chasing his tail, then tearing down
and eating some bunting.

At the end of the day, I had a twenty per cent
lead. Freddie is back.

CHUCK'S PEP TALK

So you're winning, huh? Feel like you're on top of
the mountain? Feel the wind in your hair as you look down on all
you've achieved? Well STOP IT! YOU FEEL NOTHING, DO YOU HEAR
ME? You're not at the top of the mountain yet. You're barely out
of base camp. You've got to push on, work harder, achieve more.
Achieve **AWESOMENESS**.

LOSERS' RALLY

I thought about your pep talk and realized that you're right. I can't rest on my laurels now. Yeah, a twenty per cent lead is good, but wouldn't a forty per cent lead be better?

I had the idea to hold a 'Losers' Rally' over the weekend. Because Losers' Club is fine for what it is, but the people don't come together enough. The chess kids go in one corner, the LARPers in another, the emos and goths jostle for space in the storage cupboard, the Epic Warfare kids (technically Nilesh and me, but mainly just Nilesh) hang by the computers. No one knows what anyone else is about. I thought if I could unify us, we would be a force to be reckoned with. Malvern's reign of terror would be over.

I personally invited everyone in the club to the rally. Everyone seemed pretty keen, because it was chance for them to show everyone why their thing was the best thing. Plus, it was the chance to hang out with Keith in the park, and who knows what he's going to get up to?

We met at the bandstand in the park at eleven. I borrowed a couple of big pieces of paper from school and wrote 'Losers' Rally' on them. I'd already picked up Keith. Heavy Metal Steve was confused when I came on a weekend, but was more than happy to let me borrow him for the day. Apparently, he'd been up all night helping Keith poo out a load of bunting and was shattered.

I organized an Awesome itinerary to make sure everything went off smoothly.

Losers' Rally Itinerary

10.50 a.m. Introduction by Freddie and Keith.

11 a.m. Choir sings 'Keith's Aria'.

11.10 a.m. Chess demonstration.

11.20 a.m. LARP.

11.30 a.m. Pokémon.

11.40 a.m. Emo poetry reading.

11.50 a.m. Learn to crochet.

12 p.m. Fun with bagpipes.

12.10 p.m. Knitting a hat for Keith.

12.30 p.m. (*Allowing extra time in case Keith eats the hat*) Acoustic set by goth band 'My Soul Belongs to Cthulhu'.

And do you know what, Chuck? We had so much fun. Everyone was interested in everyone else's hobbies and was so respectful. Afterwards, we even did a bit of crossover and tried each other's stuff. The goths took to LARPing like ducks to water and the emos crocheted some really profound lyrics. I left on a high, feeling like I'd climbed that mountain just a little further and nothing could possibly knock me off.

WHACK!

I fell to the ground.

I looked up, and there was Nilesh standing over me. He'd pushed me really hard and winded me. Before he could do anything else, Lee and Perry were on him, holding him back. I got up and dusted myself off.

'Oh, so that's how it is now, is it?' Nilesh yelled. 'You've got your heavies doing your dirty work for you?'

'Do you want us to do him in, boss?' said Perry.

'No,' I said. 'Let him go.'

They did as they were told and Nilesh stomped over to me and got in my face. 'Sunday the twelfth of May. That date mean anything to you?'

I searched my memory banks. 'Um, it's the first anniversary of the release of Chuck Willard's exercise DVD, 'Grin Yourself Thin'?

Nilesh growled and pushed me proper hard. 'Think again.'

I tried, I really did, but . . . Nothing.

Nilesh grabbed me by the collar and pulled me close. 'It was the Epic Warfare regional tournament.'

Oh. Ohhhh. With all the excitement of the Losers' Rally, I had forgotten all about it.

'I-I'm sorry,' I said.

'Sorry?' he hissed. 'You're sorry? Do you have any idea how humiliated I was? Two dozen Epic Warfare geeks were chanting 'She got stood up' at me. All day.

'All day?' I said.

'Yes,' he said. 'I waited for you. All. Day. I thought you must be just running late or something.'

I didn't know what to say, Chuck. I was on such a high and now Nilesh was being a downer again.

'You could have reminded me!' I said.

Nilesh stared at me as if he wanted to rip out my eyes and use them as ping-pong balls.

'I did remind you,' he growled. 'I reminded you every single day for the past month.'

'Really?' I said.

'Yes,' he said. 'It just shows how much you listen. Unless it's Chuck "stupid teeth" Willard, you don't want to know. You discovering that idiot was the worst thing that has ever happened to us.'

'Hey!' I yelled. 'Chuck Willard is NOT an idiot, he is the man who is going to help save my family!'

'Right,' said Nilesh. 'None of this is about your family and you know it. This is all about the glory.'

'What are you talking about?' I said.

'You started to get a bit of success and it went to your head,' said Nilesh. 'You've changed.'

My hands shook, my eye twitched. I tried to remember the Chuck Willard yoga mantra, but it was too late.

'So what if I have changed?' I yelled. 'I'm glad. I'm a better person now. I don't care about stupid computer games any more. Not like you. "Come and play Epic Warfare, come and play Epic Warfare." GIVE IT A REST!'

Nilesh shook his head and stared at me. When he finally spoke, it was in a really quiet voice.

'It was never about Epic Warfare, Freddie,' he said. 'It was about wanting to spend time with my best friend.'

I tried to think of something to say to that. Something devastating. But I couldn't. It was then it finally dawned on me that me and Nilesh have grown apart.

That's OK, Chuck. It's fine. It's natural. In fact, I didn't even get stressed out. I just went straight to the toilet and spent ten minutes in there not crying.

CHUCK'S PEP TALK

I'm going to tell you a story.

Once upon a time, a guy was walking through a forest, when he came upon a lion with a thorn in its paw. Taking pity on the beast, the man tenderly removed it. The lion was grateful and left him in peace.

Many years later, the man was captured and forced to be a gladiator. He was given a thin spear and told to go out and fight the lions. Not just one but five of the ferocious creatures surrounded him. The man awaited the lethal blow, but it never came. The biggest lion walked up to him and looked into his eyes. That was when the man realized it was the same lion he had helped all those years earlier. He could see that he remembered, too. The lion stepped slowly closer and the man gently touched the lion's mane in a gesture of respect.

Then the lion killed him, because he didn't want to look like a wuss in front of his buddies.

Do you see what I'm trying to tell you? In order to be Awesome, you've got to look out for number one and never lose face. If people get hurt along the way, it's collateral damage. Ya don't make an omelette without breaking a few heads.

Now make like the lion, get out there, and ROAR.

SPILLING THE BEANS

I tried to roar, Chuck, I really did.

I mean, everything's good, really. There are only five days until the election and I have a huge lead, the Losers' Club is better than ever, and Malvern seems to be in hiding. Not even his Lowes Park Bantz posts are having an effect any more.

@LOWESPARKBANTZ Smallhouse? More like SMELLhouse.

Nilesh not being around wasn't great, but then again, how much has he been around lately, anyway? Ever since I realized I had to bend the rules a little to level the playing field, he has been nothing but a drag. Without him, I'm free to do what I want. When I'm president, he'll come crawling back. And maybe I will allow him back into my circle of trust. But he'll have to earn it.

When I got home this afternoon, Dad was packing our stuff. He had started by sorting it into two piles—things we're taking with us to the B&B and things to be thrown away. And there was good stuff in the throw-away pile, Chuck—books, DVDs, games. The kinds of things there will be no room for in a poky bedroom. I couldn't take it any more. I had to give him the good news.

'What is it, son?' he said, taking his earplugs out. I didn't need to ask why he had them in. Uncle Barry was singing a German oompah song called 'Mein Schmetterling' really loudly downstairs.

'I'm winning in the election!' I said.

Dad nodded sadly. 'Well, don't get your hopes

up too much, they'll still probably win, like they always do. That's why they still have their nice house across town and we're . . . ' He stopped and looked around. 'Here.'

'Come on, Dad, be more positive,' I said. 'After all, I'm doing it for you.'

Dad stopped packing for a second and looked at me. 'What do you mean?'

'When I'm elected president, I'm going to get you a job as a teacher,' I said.

Dad's jaw dropped. 'A teacher? But I'm not even qualified!'

'That doesn't matter,' I said. 'You should see the bloke that teaches us Geography.'

'But I can't,' said Dad. 'I don't know the first thing about working in a school. I mean, I went there myself and I hated the place. I wouldn't want to go back there every day.'

It went quiet. My face felt prickly. Surely all this hadn't been for nothing?

'I'm sorry, Freddie,' said Dad.

'No, it's fine,' I squeaked. 'It's . . . it's absolutely fine.'

Needless to say, Chuck, it's not fine. Not fine at all.

DRAINED

What do I do now, Chuck? What's the point of being president when the whole reason I was doing it turns out to be a dud? What good is a president if he lives in a dump and is covered in rat poo? And I'll only have to resign when I move schools, anyway.

I just feel drained, Chuck. I've tried everything to make my dad Awesome and when I finally find something that might work, he shoots it down. It's like he doesn't want to be Awesome. I tried talking to Mum about it but she gave me a hug and said the same thing—Dad would be bad at working in a school. I don't know, I guess I thought my dad could do anything.

Normally, I'd talk to Nilesh about stuff like this, but I can't even do that now. I tried to explain it to Lee and Perry but they're not really the most sensitive types. There's only one person who can help me now: you.

I really need to speak to you in person, Chuck. I mean, the **COMPLETE ROAD TO AWESOMENESS PROGRAM** is great and everything, but it's not the same as speaking to you in person and absorbing your Awesomeness.

When I got home from school, I called your helpline, hoping that you might be there.

'Welcome . . . to . . . the . . . Chuck . . . . . . Will . . . . ard . . . help . . . . line. Calls . . . cost . . . a dollar fifty . . . a . . . minute. Tell us how . . . Chuck . . . can help . . . you . . . after . . . the . . . beep.'

BEEP

'Hi, I need to speak to Chuck.'

'You said you'd . . . like . . . to . . . buy a Chuck T-shirt. . . . . . If this is correct . . . press one. If this is . . . in . . . . correct . . . press . . . two.'

Well, Chuck, it went on like that until Uncle Barry came in and caught me, then had to lie down in a darkened room when he found out how much it had cost. So I was truly stuck. We're getting kicked out in three days, so it's kind of urgent.

Then an alert came up on the
AWESOMENESS APP.

×

Hey there, UK Awesomers. I'm heading to your shores right now! My tour kicks off on Thursday night at the Birmingham MegaDome. If you don't have tickets, it's tough luck, cos it's SOLD OUT!

Right then, I knew what I had to do, Chuck. I had to come and speak to you. Like I said before, I couldn't get tickets, but stuff like that can be worked out later. You are my family's last hope. Please don't let me down.

THE MISSION

It's the day before the election and what a day
it has been, Chuck. Malvern had shifted up his
campaigning a gear, putting up posters all over
school that said, 'Vote for Malvern—The ONLY
candidate endorsed by a REAL celebrity.'

I couldn't concentrate on any of that, though.
All I did was go over the facts—I have no best
friend and soon, I'll have no home. The election
just didn't matter to me any more. I didn't
even bother bringing Keith in this morning.
I just walked him and took him home. The
Losers' Club would be disappointed, but they'd
understand.

At break, I got my tablet out and checked
your Twitter feed.

@ChuckWillard Checking into the Awesome
Birmingham MegaDome early. Great place!

That settled it. I had to act immediately. I headed straight out of school without telling anyone, and ran as fast as I could to the train station. I knew I would get a report for leaving school without permission, but I didn't care. It's like you say, Chuck, sometimes you have to prioritize.

I checked the board and saw that a train calling at the airport, which is right over the road from the MegaDome, was arriving in a couple of minutes.

As I got on, I thought about what I would say to you. Maybe I would ask you for advice. Maybe I would ask you to give my dad a job in your organization, like the head of your Tammerstone chapter or something.

'Excuse me, young man?'

I shook my head and snapped back to reality. Standing over me was the conductor.

'Can I see your ticket, please?'

Oh no.

I winced a little. 'I, um, lost it.'

The conductor chuckled to herself. 'Of course

you did. I'm going to need to take your address, please.'

I went to argue, but then stopped. By the time they sent the fine through the post, we'd be out of there, anyway. I gave her Uncle Barry's address and she went on her way.

I pulled out my tablet. I had tons of notifications.

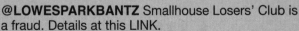

@LOWESPARKBANTZ Smallhouse Losers' Club is a fraud. Details at this LINK.

Even though I really didn't want to, I clicked the link.

In an explosive turn of events, it has been revealed that Freddie Smallhouse actually HATES the members of his so-called 'Losers' Club'. Listen to this exclusive recording.

What recording? I clicked and listened.

'I don't REALLY care about these people. I'm just doing it to help me win.'

WHAT? I didn't say that! I said I didn't care about chess! He must have bugged the library because he knew I was using it as my campaign HQ, then edited it to make me look bad. And I do care about chess now. After the Losers' Rally, I care about all of it. This is so unfair! Thinking back, that's how he must have been one step ahead of me for so long. He was listening to what we were saying. I guess it's like Dad said, Chuck. The Popes always win.

It meant that this meeting-you plan really had to work. If it failed, I had nothing.

When the train pulled into the station, I followed the signs for the MegaDome until I found myself in the car park. A massive billboard with your face on looked back at me.

My mouth was as dry as an old flip-flop and my belly was filled with a million hyperactive butterflies. I glanced up at the MegaDome, all silver and curved like a giant spaceship. I guess you have to play places like that because anywhere smaller wouldn't be able to contain all your Awesomeness.

The area around the arena was pretty quiet. The only person I came across was this dirty looking bloke asking if I had tickets I wanted to sell him. Yeah right, mate. If I had tickets for a Chuck show, I wouldn't let you anywhere near them. Never trust anyone with more tattoos on their face than teeth in their mouth, that's my motto.

I consulted a big signpost map and eventually found the VIP entrance. It was being guarded by this enormous bouncer that made Lee and Perry look like a pair of fluffy kittens.

I stopped and took a deep breath. He puts his pants on one leg at a time. One giant leg at a time.

I walked up to him as confidently as I could, trying to remember all I learned from your 'Walk Like a Winner' video. Legs apart, shoulders back, head high.

'Toilets are that way,' said the bouncer, pointing around the corner.

I was confused. 'Um, I don't need the toilet,' I said.

'Oh,' said the bouncer. 'I just assumed from how you were walking, you'd had an accident.'

I grimaced. Not the best start.

'I'm here to see Chuck,' I said, my voice going up at the end for some reason, making it sound like a question.

The guard raised an eyebrow. 'You got an appointment?'

'Well . . . no,' I said. 'But I am part of the program.'

'Part of the what?'

'The program,' I said. 'You know, the **COMPLETE ROAD TO AWESOMENESS PROGRAM**? I'm sure Chuck will be glad to see me.'

The bouncer chuckled and said, 'If you don't have an appointment or a VIP pass, you're not coming in.'

'But it's really important that I speak to him,' I said. 'Life or death.'

He just glared.

My mouth flapped like I was a goldfish that jumped out of the bowl. I wanted to get across how important this was, but I couldn't make the words come out.

'Honestly,' I said. 'I—I'm his biggest fan. I know everything about him.'

'Except for the fact that he doesn't want you backstage without an invite,' said the bouncer. 'Now please leave the area.'

'But—' I cut in.

'Leave. The. Area,' he said, curling his massive hand into a fist the size of an iceberg lettuce.

I left the area.

So I was stuck, Chuck. I needed to speak to you more than anything in the world and I had no way of getting in. Every entrance would be staffed with monsters like that. That was when I turned around and saw the face-tattoo man.

'You OK, kid?' he said. 'Wanna sell a ticket?'

'No,' I said. 'I need a ticket.'

His spider-webbed face cracked into a grin. 'Well, why didn't you say so?'

He shuffled over to me and pulled a ticket out of his top pocket. 'This little beauty is in the third row,' he said.

'OK,' I said. 'How much?'

The man's piggy eyes narrowed. 'Two hundred quid.'

Honestly, Chuck, I nearly fainted. You know as well as I do, the stalls seats for your Birmingham MegaDome show cost from £65 to £95.

'What?' I cried. 'Why is it that much?'

'Sold out show, little pal,' said the man with a throaty chuckle. 'Supply and demand.'

I sighed. 'But I haven't got that kind of money.'

The man pocketed the ticket and nodded. 'OK. Have a good evening.'

He started to walk away, but I called him back. He smiled like a cartoon cat that had just set a trap.

I reached into my bag and pulled out my tablet. 'Would you take this as payment?'

He grabbed it and turned it over in his hands. 'It's not even a year old,' I said. 'And it's worth more than two hundred.'

The man pressed the ON button to make sure it worked and looked it over like my Dad used to do with antiques. Finally, he nodded and said, 'You've got yourself a deal.'

He dropped my tablet into his bag and handed me the ticket. 'Enjoy,' he said.

I had this horrible numb feeling in my stomach, but I tried to ignore it and concentrate on what I had to do. I walked around the edge of the MegaDome until I found the main entrance. There were already a few people about, presumably here early to take a look around Chuck's Exhibition of Awesomeness—a portable museum dedicated to how Awesome you are.

I showed the man my ticket and thankfully, it must have been real because he allowed me in. Inside, it was as Mega as the name suggested. There were signs everywhere—'Gates 23-27 This Way', 'Gates 28-32 This Way'. It was more like an airport than a concert venue. The sheer size

of it meant I had no idea how to get to you. All
the doors to the main auditorium were locked.
I decided to turn left and go backwards through
the numbers, past row after row of fast food stalls
and merchandise counters. I really liked the look
of your official T-shirt.

I kept walking until I was past Gate 1. Sure
enough, there was a set of double doors, guarded

by a bouncer just as huge as the one at the VIP entrance.

'Can I help you?' he said.

This time, I didn't even bother trying to talk my way in as a member of the program. I was going to have to lie, or as you put it, Chuck, 'get freaky with the truth'.

'I'm the competition winner,' I said.

The bouncer frowned. 'What competition?'

I cleared my throat, tried to look him in the eye, but then wussed out and stared at the control panel next to his head.

'The, um, you know, meet Chuck competition.'

'What's your name?' he asked. 'I'll see if you're on the guest list.'

Come on, Freddie, think. What would someone on Chuck Willard's guest list be called?

'Jeff . . . erson,' I started. 'Mc . . . Yankee . . . ford?'

The bouncer raised his eyebrows at me and smirked. 'Nice try, kid.'

No. This couldn't be it. I had to get in there and see you. There was no way I could just turn around and go. Without thinking, I crumpled to the ground and lolled my tongue out of the side of my mouth.

The bouncer leaned over me. 'Are you OK?' he said.

I said nothing, just stared into space and tried to make my eyes as glazed as possible.

'Kid?'

I allowed myself a super croaky groan.

The bouncer swore under his breath, then turned back to the door. He stopped at the control panel and I made sure I was watching.

2...9...3...3...1

Then he opened the door and ran inside. As soon as he'd gone, I leapt to my feet, entered the code and went in. I saw the bouncer running off ahead, shouting into his walkie-talkie. I knew he'd be back straight away, so I opened the nearest door and leapt inside. It was obviously some kind of cleaners' cupboard so I curled myself into a ball and hid behind a big vacuum cleaner. I heard two pairs of footsteps running back and the door opening.

'I swear he was here a second ago,' the bouncer said.

'Are you alright, Dave?' said another voice. 'Not cracking up, are you?'

'He was here,' the bouncer insisted. 'Well, I thought he was.'

The other man laughed. 'Maybe it was a ghost.'

'Shut up,' said the bouncer, deadly seriously. 'Don't even joke about things like that.'

When it felt safe, I crept out of my hiding place and made my way down the corridor. Even though I was deadly serious about finding you, I still couldn't help but be amazed by the backstage area and imagine all the mega-famous people that had been there.

I walked past loads of people, but they were all rushing around and didn't even notice me. Still, I couldn't ask someone where your dressing room was because that might give me away. I scouted around every corridor, even cut through the catering area, until I found it.

Chuck
WILLARD
DO NOT DISTURB.

I went to knock the door but I couldn't bring myself to do it. My fist froze. I couldn't really talk to you, could I? You're a famous superstar and I'm . . . well, I'm me. It would be ridiculous. I went to walk away. But then I stopped. No. I couldn't come this far and then chicken out. That would be the most unAwesome thing ever.

'It'll be fine,' I said to myself. 'Chuck will take one look at me and see a kindred spirit. I bet it'll be like seeing his younger self. When I leave this room, my life is going to be changed forever.'

I quickly knocked, before I could talk myself out of it.

I waited. And waited.

I knocked again, this time louder. Still no response.

I tried the handle. It opened and I slowly pushed the door.

Your dressing room was amazing, Chuck. Everything was either deep black or gleaming white. There was a big, luxurious sofa against the wall, and there were flowers everywhere. A long rack of expensive-looking suits stood at the other end of the room. It sounds weird, Chuck, but I could actually feel the Awesomeness in the air. I even tried to breathe it in.

My Awesome inhalation attempt was interrupted by a shout from outside the door.

'WHAT IS YOUR FREAKING PROBLEM?'

Oh no. I quickly scrambled behind the suit rack and crouched. Whoever that was probably wouldn't be happy to find me in Chuck's dressing room.

The door flew open and smacked against the wall as the tirade continued.

'I don't want to hear your lame excuses,

Courtney. I refuse to eat the slop this crudhole has provided. Now somewhere in this backwater, hillbilly town has to have fresh kale, so do your job and find it or I'll fire you and have you on the first plane back to Palookaville!'

'Y-yes, Chuck.'

CHUCK?!

'What did you just call me?'

'Mr Willard. Mr Willard. Sir.'

'That's better. Now get the hell out of here.'

This couldn't be right. This is not how Chuck Willard speaks to his employees. I mean, you said so yourself, 'Be Awesome to everyone.' You were definitely not Awesome to that lady.

Now this was an awkward situation, Chuck. What was I supposed to do, just walk out and say hi? Yell 'SURPRISE!?'

'This is the worst country on God's green earth, I swear,' you said to yourself. 'The food here isn't fit for a dog.'

Your phone rang. Your ringtone was the theme to your short-lived gameshow, 'Try Your Luck with Chuck'.

'What do you want?' you snapped. 'Oh yeah, the stupid radio promo thing. Right, give me a sec to get in the zone.'

You got up and started pacing around. Oh God, this is not good. I was scared my heart was beating so fast that you would hear it.

'Hey, this is Chuck Willard and you're listening to Birmingham Radio—the most Awesome sounds in the most Awesome city. If you want to hear the rockingest, rollingest, red hot tracks, keep that dial locked to Birmingham R—AAAAAARRRGGGGHHH!'

Yeah, you found me. To be honest, Chuck, I thought you'd have been calmer about it.

'Stay back,' you screamed. 'All I have to do is press my alarm and my guys will be in here, folding you up into tiny pieces and mailing you to Siberia.'

'Please, Mr Willard,' I said, putting my hands up like the police had their guns trained on me. 'I'm your biggest fan.'

You backed slowly towards your dresser and picked up a hairdryer. 'What do you want?' you whispered, holding it like a pistol.

You were a lot smaller in the flesh than you looked on TV. And up close, you had wrinkles and bags under your eyes. I'd never noticed them before.

'I-I need your help,' I said. 'My family's about to be kicked out of our house and I'm desperate.'

'So that's what this is?' you said. 'A shakedown? You're going to regret this.' You reached under your shirt and pulled out a button attached to a necklace.

'Please, Mr Willard,' I said. 'I've been part of your program for ages. You've changed my life.'

'Yeah, you and a million others, so freaking what?' you sneered.

I couldn't believe it, Chuck. After watching you for so many hours, being Awesome on TV, this was like being kicked in the face. If I couldn't trust Chuck, who could I trust?

'I-I'm sorry Mr Willard,' I said.

'"I'm sorry Mr Willard",' you whimpered, mimicking me. 'Seriously, the British are nothing but a bunch of lily-livered losers. And so pale. Do yourself a favour, kid. Move to a country that isn't ninety-five per cent rain.'

I gulped. I had to try and remember why I was there.

'Look, Mr Willard,' I said. 'I don't want your money. I just want some advice.'

'Well, you're in luck,' you said. 'Because advice is what I do. You can find it in any of my reasonably-priced books and DVDs.'

'But Mr Willard—' I started, but you cut me off making a weird, squeaky noise which I think was supposed to be me.

'Meh meh meh meh meh,' you went. 'That's all I'm hearing right now.'

'But—'

'Meh meh meh!'

'Mr—'

Every time I tried to speak, you'd cut me off making that noise. It was horrible, like my whole world had been turned upside down. How could the most Awesome person in the world be so unAwesome?

'You're not going to help me, are you?' I said.

You smiled, then pressed the button on your pendant. 'Nope,' you said.

After being roughly manhandled out of the MegaDome by the guard who thought I was a ghost, my ticket was confiscated, which meant I couldn't even try and trade my tablet back with old Spiderface, and I headed back to the station.

By the time I got back to Tammerstone, I was on the verge of tears. Everything was ruined. Nothing could save my family and my campaign was over. And you, Chuckerston W. Willard are a massive fraud.

ELECTION DAY

'Wakey wakey, rise and shine!'

I shot up in bed. Uncle Barry was stomping along the landing, smacking a saucepan with a wooden spoon.

Mum, Dad, and I emerged and were led downstairs by Uncle Barry, still banging the pan.

'Good morning, family!' he said. 'I have taken the liberty of loading up all your things.' He pointed at a big blue van, parked outside. 'It didn't take long, what with you not having much.'

Dad rubbed his eyes. 'But it's half six!'

'That is correct, my dear brother-in-law,' said Uncle Barry. 'But the Turkletons are very keen to get in and start conducting their séances, and I have a Stuttgart-bound plane to catch.'

'But where are we going?' Mum asked.

'I've used my connections at the council to secure you a wonderful dwelling,' he said. 'A marvellous little place called Eden House.'

Eden House? Sounded nice. How could something named after the Garden of Eden be bad?

Well, when we got there, I guessed it must have been named after some other kind of Eden. Where instead of an apple tree, there was a smashed phone box, and instead of grassy meadows, there was a weed-choked yard with a stained mattress in it, and instead of Adam and Eve there were two old men fighting over a Pot Noodle.

'I'm sure it's much nicer on the inside,' said Mum.

Once the owner of Eden House, a delightful gent affectionately known as 'Trevor the Git', showed us to our room, Mum was very quickly proven wrong. Our entire living space was about the same size as Mum and Dad's old bedroom, with a double bed against one wall and a single against the other. The flowery wallpaper that looked like it was probably put up to celebrate the end of World War One was peeling off the walls, and a single window, thick with grime, overlooked a cluster of overflowing bins.

'We can make the best of it,' said Mum, her voice all wobbly. 'And besides, it's only temporary.'

I looked at Dad, but he just stood at the window watching those two men from before doing WWE moves on each other.

'How temporary?' I asked.

Mum straightened up her duvet. 'A few weeks,' she said. 'Definitely no longer than a month. Or two.'

I gulped down a lump in my throat. 'And then what?'

'Well, Uncle Barry said there is a shortage of council houses in Tammerstone, so we might have to move over to Pondside,' she said.

'Pondside?' I cried. 'We can't go there! I'll be eaten alive!'

Pondside is about fifteen miles away. You always hear about it on the local news, usually along with phrases like 'police siege' and 'mass arrests' and 'riot in Lidl'.

'Never mind that,' she said. 'Go down the hall

to the bathroom and fill the kettle. I think we could all do with a cup of tea.'

I took the tiny plastic kettle along the corridor and tried the bathroom door. It was locked, but a couple of seconds later, it opened and the biggest, hairiest man I've seen in my life waddled out, with a newspaper under his arm.

'I'd stay out of trap one for five minutes, if I were you,' he said.

I didn't know what he meant, but the eye-watering odour beat me out of there like roaring flames. Then I went to the bathroom on the floor below and found the sink full of cockroaches.

'So, this is home,' I said to myself.

THE VOTE

I didn't want to go to school after that, but Mum insisted. I guess she was right. Why would I want to spend any longer in that place than was necessary? I imagined thousands of fleas burrowing into my skin and I kept scratching myself all over like Keith did after he ran through that nettle patch.

We were all led down to the theatre for the final ceremony before the election. I made eye contact with a few members of the Losers' Club but they either blanked me or swore at me. Who could blame them? They all thought I didn't even like them and was only using them to win the election. I thought about trying to explain myself, but what would be the point?

Apparently, we were supposed to make a final speech before everyone could cast their votes. I had completely forgotten about it, to be honest. I suppose homelessness will do that.

I sat on a chair on the stage next to Malvern. He side-eyed me smugly and said, 'Ready to lose, chump?'

I ignored him. Why should I waste my energy getting upset by him? I had bigger concerns. In fact, why bother even going up for election? Even if I pulled off a miracle and won, who would respect a president who has to share a bathroom with a bloke called 'Hairy Dave'?

That was when I made up my mind. I was going to use my speech to withdraw and give the presidency to Malvern by default. It's like Dad said, 'The Popes always win.'

After Mr Bümfacé gave an introduction, Malvern stood up, turned to me and whispered, 'Watch this, loser.'

'Listen up,' he said, leaning on the lectern as he spoke. 'You're going to vote for me and you know it. I have always been top of the pile here so why don't we just make it official? Even if Smallhouse was sincere about speaking up for you losers, which, as we've heard, he most definitely isn't, it wouldn't matter, because you need someone

★ 246 ★

popular and smart and handsome to be your leader. In short, you need me.'

With that, he walked back to his seat to a huge round of applause. I noticed Malvern Sr giving him a standing ovation from the front row. He tried to start a 'Malvern' chant but it didn't really work.

Mr Bümfacé gave me a nod and I walked up to total silence. I took a deep breath and blinked hard. After working so hard, it was sad to be quitting at the last minute, but it was the best thing to do. At least Malvern wouldn't have the satisfaction of beating me.

'Hello everyone,' I said. 'I know this is supposed to be my big speech where I convince you that I deserve your vote. But the truth is, I don't. I have decided to withdraw from—'

'Wait!' I heard a voice behind me. 'Don't do it.'

I turned around and saw Dad walking towards me. He was wearing his best suit, which I didn't even know he'd kept.

'What are you doing here?' I whispered.

He stepped up next to me so he could speak

into the mic.

'Hello, boys and girls,' he said. 'You don't know me—I'm Freddie's dad. I'm just here to tell you that my son is the best.'

I went bright red, partly because I was embarrassed and partly because I never thought I'd hear my dad say anything like that about me again.

'He might not be the most popular, or clever, or good-looking,' he went on, 'and yes, maybe his eyes are too close together, but he is the best president you could wish for.' He stopped and took a shaky breath. 'Today, I am ashamed to say, my family has become homeless. We're now living in a grotty B&B called Eden House. And it's all my fault. Now, in the past few weeks, Freddie has worked tirelessly to stop this from happening. He has tried so many different things, even taking part in this election. While I gave up and resigned myself and my family to a life of misery, he wouldn't take it, and fought against it. This is who you want as your leader—someone with guts and determination. Someone who'll fight for you.'

Colin Roctor stood up. 'Excuse me,' he said. 'but Freddie said he didn't care about any of us and was using us to win the election.'

Dad nodded. 'I'm glad you brought that up, young man,' he said. 'Because I was just about to address that very point.' He gestured up at the sound box at the top of the theatre. 'Nilesh, play the tape.'

I looked up there, and sure enough, there was Nilesh. A second later I heard my own voice coming over the PA.

'I don't REALLY care about chess and board games or whatever they're all into, but I do care about the people. If I can hear their concerns, I can win them over and it will help me win.'

'Listen. If we mobilize all the types of people Malvern wouldn't let into his precious celebrity party, we can take it. Imagine this school with the losers running the show. It'll turn it on its head!'

A gasp went across the crowd. Malvern looked like he was going to explode.

'This morning, I left the B&B I now call home and went for a walk back to my old neighbourhood,' Dad said. 'That was where I saw Nilesh. We got to talking about the election campaign and how much effort Freddie had put into it. Then he told me that Malvern bugged the library and used an Instagram account to try and sway the election.'

'Lies!' Malvern shrieked, leaping to his feet. 'I hope you have proof of this OUTRAGEOUS accusation.'

Without turning around, Dad reached into his pocket and pulled out a mic with 'PROPERTY OF MALVERN POPE' written on it. 'Nilesh found this behind some books on a shelf,' he said.

'Curse that infernal label maker,' Malvern hissed.

'No matter what happens today,' said Dad. 'Malvern will be going home to a nice house with his own bedroom. Freddie won't. So you have one choice: reward dishonesty and give Malvern yet another privilege, or help Freddie out for trying his best. Thank you.'

A small applause started at the front of the room, which spread to the back, then got louder and louder, until it was a standing ovation. I stood next to Dad and watched. It was amazing.

'Thanks,' I said to him.

Dad put his arm around me and squeezed. 'It was the least I could do,' he said. 'I should have believed in you sooner. When Nilesh told me everything you had done, it was like a big splash of cold water in my face. It made me realize what I could achieve if I put my mind to it. What I'm trying to say is, you inspired me to be Awesome, Freddie.'

I cringed. 'Yeah, I'm not so sure about Awesomeness anymore. I don't think Chuck is as great as he makes out.'

Dad shook his head. 'I'm not talking about Chuck,' he said. 'I always knew he was a huckster. You're the Awesome one, son. You did all this, not Chuck.'

'Really?' I said.

'Yes!' said Dad. 'You don't need some massive-toothed moron to tell you how to be amazing, because you already are.'

Did you hear that, Chuck? I've been Awesome

all along. I hope your assistant farted in your kale.

While the votes were being counted, I headed up the stairs to the sound booth. I found Nilesh in there, sitting down, staring out the window at the stage.

'Um, hello Nilesh,' I said.

'Hello,' he replied, flatly.

'I didn't know you knew how to work all this,' I said, gesturing at the bank of buttons. 'Looks complicated.'

Nilesh shrugged, still looking out at the theatre. 'I thought about what you said about Epic Warfare being a waste of time. Made me realize I should learn some useful skills.'

I sighed. 'I'm sorry for saying that,' I said. 'I didn't mean it.'

Nilesh didn't say anything.

'So how come you decided to help me?' I said.

'Well, I spoke to your dad,' he said. 'Plus, I don't agree with what Malvern has done. I hate cheating, regardless of who's doing it.'

It went quiet for a while. I couldn't think of anything to say. Until I remembered the thing I still needed to say.

'I'm sorry I didn't show up to the tournament.'

Nilesh turned around in his chair. 'Really?'

I nodded. 'I just got so crazy trying to stop my family becoming homeless, I forgot everything else.'

'Understandable, I guess,' he said. 'Your dad told me about your new place. Sounds grim.'

'Yeah,' I said. 'Kind of is.'

Nilesh stood up and walked over to me. 'Friends now?' He stuck his hand out.

I smiled and shook his hand. 'Friends,' I said.

THE RESULT

We were all called back into the hall for the result. We had to sit back down on the chairs on stage. Malvern was smiling as charmingly as he could, but his eyes were pure psycho-killer.

'Well, ladies and gentlemen,' said Mr Bümfacé. 'This has been a long, hard, brutal campaign. To be honest, I didn't realize it was going to be like this. If I had, I'd have probably just held a readathon or something like that. Anyway, what's done is done. Now is the moment we have all been waiting for. The results of the election.'

He held up an envelope. It wasn't gold and sparkly like you have at awards ceremonies. It was brown and had a coffee ring on it.

'And the winner of the Lowes Park Presidential Election is . . .'

He opened the envelope and I held my breath. The room fell silent. I looked at the back of the room. Dad sat on the step, leaning forwards, his fingers interlocked as if he were praying. Nilesh came out of the box and stood in the doorway. Malvern Sr stared straight ahead, but it was hard to tell what he was thinking, under his shades.

'Freddie Smallhouse of the Awesomeness Party!'

The hall erupted with cheers. Malvern stood up and screamed, 'NOOOOOOOO!' Before I could do anything, the entire Losers' Club stormed the stage and lifted me as high as their PE-dodging arms could.

'FRED-DIE! FRED-DIE!' they chanted.

I'm not going to lie, it was a pretty cool moment. And it was even better because I'd done it honestly. In the end, anyway. We'll ignore the whole 'pretend Keith is Mittens' fiasco.

They carried me around the stage and chanted until Mr Bümfacé could finally get back control. I gave a victory speech where I thanked Dad and Nilesh, but I can't really remember what I said. It was all a massive blur. It felt like something had really changed. Like maybe the kids that call us names and trip us up in the corridors aren't that powerful after all. It might turn out to be nothing, of course, but right now, it feels pretty Awesome.

When it had finished, Dad came up and gave me a hug. 'I'm so proud of you,' he said.

'I couldn't have done it without your speech,' I replied.

Dad shook his head. 'Don't be daft. You did this all yourself and you handled it with class. Speaking of which.'

Malvern Sr stalked over and stared at us

through his shades. 'That was a low trick, Smallhouse,' he said.

'What? Pointing out the fact that your boy's a cheat?' said Dad.

Malvern Sr's jaw tightened and he straightened his tie. 'You haven't heard the last of this, do you understand me?'

Dad smiled. 'Don't be like that, Malvern. It's business, remember? It's like you always said, 'If you want to get ahead in business, you've got to play dirty sometimes.' He held out his hand. 'Now put her there.'

Malvern Sr reluctantly went to take Dad's hand, but then Dad quickly drew it back, thumbed his nose and said 'Psyche!'

I laughed super hard. Dad hasn't done that in so long. It felt like I had finally got the old him back. The problem was, as soon as we went back to Eden House, Old Dad would go away again. This would be a temporary high, soon replaced by ugly reality.

We were sitting in Eden House later on, wondering if it was safe to leave the room or whether the screamy, sweary, almost-naked man was still on the loose, when Trevor the Git banged on the door.

'Which one of you's Freddie?' he grunted.

I reluctantly said it was me. For all I knew he could have been trying to recruit me for some kind of illegal boxing club in the basement.

He wiped his nose with the back of his hand and threw a phone at me. 'S-for you,' he said.

I put the grimy phone to my ear and said hello.

'Hi Freddie, it's Bridget Meyers from the mathletics club.'

Weird. She'd never called me before. Maybe she wanted to congratulate me on winning the election.

'I remember your dad saying something about Eden House in his speech and I looked up the number,' she went on. 'The receptionist seems . . . interesting.'

I would have used a better word to describe Trevor the Git, but he was staring at me from the doorway with his beefy arms folded.

'Anyway, the reason I'm calling is my mum

runs a company that employs motivational speakers, and I told her about your dad's speech earlier and she said she'd like to meet him,' Bridget explained.

My eyes must have gone all big because Mum and Dad looked at me as if they wanted to know what was happening.

'So you're saying she might give him a job?' I said.

'He'll have to be interviewed, but if it goes well . . . yes. How about I pass the phone over to my mum and you pass the phone over to your dad, and they can sort something out?'

I handed Dad the phone. 'What's this about?' he said to me. 'Good news I hope?'

'Not just good news,' I said. 'Awesome news.'

THE END

I think this is going to be my last entry in the Journal of Awesomeness, Chuck. Meeting you for real kind of took the shine off. No offence.

Not that you care. I suppose you have enough to worry about now your assistant has finally had enough of your meanness and leaked a recording of you screaming at her because your coffee was a degree too hot. Seems like a lot of people don't think you're so Awesome any more.

Anyway, Dad absolutely aced his interview, as I knew he would, and Bridget's mum gave him an advance on his salary so we could get out of Eden House and check into a much nicer hotel. I mean, a much nicer hotel would be a box with half a sandwich in it, but you get the idea. We've found a new house and we're going to move in, in a couple of weeks. It's not far from where we used to live and even closer to Nilesh's, which is even better.

Dad loves his new job. He made it clear to them that he wouldn't be talking any Chuck Willard-style mumbo jumbo (again, no offence) but would be talking about his own life experiences and how he hit the bottom and came back.

I still walk Keith every day before and after school, and he even sometimes comes in and joins the Losers' Club at lunchtime. The club pretty much runs itself these days, but Nilesh and I go and play games together from time to time.

I thought it would be loads of work being president, but it's not really. It's mainly going out and doing the tombola at old folks' homes to try and prove that not everyone from Lowes Park is a hooligan. The only thing I really get to decide is where we go on our school trip.

LOWES PARK

HIGH SCHOOL

TRIP TO . . .

CON

Well, it's the least I could do.

I'd better stop there. Nilesh called about five minutes ago.

'Oh my God,' he said. 'The Barringtons are having a church committee meeting in their living room and one of the music channels is showing wall-to-wall hardcore gangsta rap. Are you up for some fun?'

'Yes,' I said. 'That sounds **AWESOME.**'

ABOUT THE AUTHOR

As well as writing books, Ben Davis has had a variety of jobs, including joke writer, library assistant, and postman. Writing books has proven the most fun.

Ben lives in Tamworth, Staffordshire, and in his spare time enjoys rock climbing, white water rafting, and pretending to have adventurous hobbies.

MORE BRILLIANTLY FUNNY BOOKS FROM BEN DAVIS

You might want to try reading one of these other **AWESOME** books. I'm afraid they don't have me in them, but hey, you can't win 'em all . . .

FULLY CHARGED AND READY FOR ACTION

ELECTRIGIRL

Written by JO COTTERILL
Illustrated by CATHY BRETT

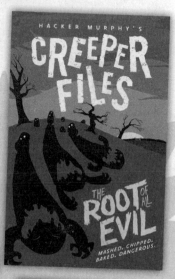

HACKER MURPHY'S

CREEPER FILES

THE ROOT OF ALL EVIL

MASHED. CHIPPED. BAKED. DANGEROUS.

ELAINE WICKSON she wrote it
CHRIS JUDGE He did the pictures

PLANET STAN

MY LIFE IN PIE CHARTS

Random mates
Level 5 humiliation
Snail carnage
Beetroot cake of doom
Utter brother chaos
A NORMAL LIFE!!!

THE Accidental BILLIONAIRE

MEET JASPER SPAM: INVENTOR OF THE CAT-CHAT 2000!

Tom McLaughlin